Dear Reader,

So many of you wrote suggesting that Logan Bruno deserved a story of his own, that I decided to take your advice. Here is a special edition BSC book, a story about Logan. I hope you enjoy it!

— Ann M Martin

**Other books by
Ann M. Martin**

Ma and Pa Dracula
Yours Turly, Shirley
Ten Kids, No Pets
Slam Book
Just a Summer Romance
Missing Since Monday
With You and Without You
Me and Katie (the Pest)
Stage Fright
Inside Out
Bummer Summer

BABY-SITTERS LITTLE SISTER series
THE BABY-SITTERS CLUB series
(see back of the book for a complete listing)

Logan's Story

Ann M. Martin

AN
APPLE
PAPERBACK

SCHOLASTIC INC.
New York Toronto London Auckland Sydney

*The author gratefully acknowledges
Peter Lerangis
for his help in
preparing this manuscript.*

Cover art by Hodges Soileau

ISBN 0-590-45575-3

12 11 10 9 8 7 6 5 4 3 2 1   2 3 4 5 6 7/9

Printed in the U.S.A.   40

First Scholastic printing, June 1992

CHAPTER 1

"Hey, Bruno, you okay?" Clarence King asked, bending over me.

I lay on the grass, holding my head. It felt as if it had been taken off and then put on backward.

"You know, King," I said, trying to smile, "this is a practice, not the Super Bowl. You didn't have to tackle me so hard."

"Sorry." King smiled and reached down to help me. "Guess I'm stronger than I think, huh?"

I like King, but modesty is not one of his strong points. (Neither is a sense of humor — just watch the smoke come out of his ears if you call him "Clarence.")

As I got to my feet, I could hear Coach Mills call out, "Look alive, you two!"

I trotted toward the line of scrimmage, feeling a little wobbly . . . and suddenly looking forward to the end of the season.

Now, don't get me wrong. I like football a lot. But some guys play as if there are NFL scouts hanging out at every practice. As for me, well, I'm in it for the fun. That's the way I run my life. Do what you enjoy, I always say. Even if people think you're a little weird. Even if they make fun of you and call you a girl, just because . . .

Whoa. I'm getting ahead of myself. Sometimes I do that — just steamroll on without realizing it. Maybe I should slow down and start from the beginning.

First of all, my name is Logan Bruno.

Second of all, I'm a guy.

Duh, no kidding, right? Well, believe it or not, sometimes people can't tell from a name like Logan. Anyway, the fact that I'm a guy is crucial to this story, so I should say it right out.

Let's see, what else do you need to know about me. . . .

I'm thirteen, and I'm in eighth grade at Stoneybrook Middle School (SMS) in Stoneybrook, Connecticut. Originally I'm from Louisville, Kentucky — and according to some people, I *sound* like it. I get teased for my drawl, but my so-called accent sounds pretty normal to me. I'm always amazed at how strange *northerners* talk. Fast, fast, fast, like there's some kind of time limit on sentences.

You probably already guessed my main interest is sports. Well, *three* of my main interests are football, baseball, and track. Not that I'm a stereotypical jock. I don't eat steaks for breakfast, grunt when I talk, or have trouble counting past my own weight. (Actually, I don't know any athletes like that . . . although King comes close.) I don't even look very jockish. I'm average height and I have an average build. My hair is blondish brown and my eyes are blue. Mary Anne Spier, my girlfriend, says I look like Cam Geary, this movie star, but she's *definitely* exaggerating.

As for Mary Anne, well, she's the other main interest in my life. Oops, wait a minute, that sounds terrible. I didn't mean *other*. It's just that I've been involved in sports longer, so . . . oh, you know what I mean. Just don't tell Mary Anne I said that. She's *very* sensitive. In fact, her sensitivity and shyness are the coolest things about her. I'm just the opposite — a take-charge kind of person, sometimes even bullheaded. You might think that would create personality problems between us. Well, you're right. We've had our ups and downs. We even broke up for awhile, because Mary Anne felt I was stifling her. I used to decide everything—when and where we were going on a date, what movies we would see, what we'd eat. I wouldn't pay attention to

Mary Anne's baby-sitting schedule or even *ask* her if she wanted to go somewhere. I just assumed.

It's not that I was being a jerk. Like I said, she's very shy, and sometimes I didn't know what she was thinking. So I figured she would be happy to let me make the decisions. Anyway, things kind of blew up. I began getting impatient with her shyness, she began resenting my forcefulness. It was a real mess. She ended up breaking it off. It was tough for both of us, but I think the time off helped. When we got around to talking again, we really figured things out. We started seeing each other again, and now we're getting along better than ever.

Maybe you noticed I mentioned Mary Anne's baby-sitting schedule. That's a big part of her life. In case you didn't know, she and her friends belong to this group called the Baby-sitters Club.

Now, a lot of people think the Baby-sitters Club is all girls. I mean, when *you* think of a baby-sitter, you think of a girl, right? Admit it. But it's sort of like the stereotype of jocks. It just doesn't make sense. Guys can take care of kids, too. They can play games and pick up toys and give baths and make dinner — no big deal. I have a younger brother and sister and I baby-sit for them a lot.

Anyway, that's a roundabout way of getting to the next important thing about myself.

I, Logan Bruno, also belong to the Baby-sitters Club.

Sort of.

I'm an associate member, which means I don't go to regular meetings or pay dues. I just fill in when things get busy.

I hope it doesn't sound like I'm *ashamed* of belonging to the BSC, because I'm not. It's just that, well, I've had to take a little razzing about it from some of my friends.

A little? OK — a lot!

Actually, it wasn't so bad at first. Most of the guys didn't even know I had this "secret life" as a baby-sitter. And besides, I wasn't needed too much by the club, so I could always work my sitting jobs around my practice schedule. I like kids a lot, so it was fun and easy.

Until recently, that is. Everything changed on that fateful day Clarence King almost knocked my head off.

Looking back, I should have taken that as an omen.

The rest of practice that day was pretty normal. King managed to behave like a human, and I even caught a twenty-seven-yard pass for a touchdown in an intrasquad game.

When it was four-thirty, Coach Mills blew

his whistle and yelled, "Head to the showers, boys! See you Tuesday, same time, same station!" (Coach Mills loves clichés.)

I saw my friend Austin Bentley trudging toward the sidelines. (Talk about names —can you imagine being named after two cars? I have to hand it to Austin. He just laughs when people tease him about it.) His practice uniform was filthy and he was walking with a slight limp. "Austin!" I called out. "You been mud wrestling or something?"

Austin turned around and gave me a mock-angry look. "No, I haven't been moooo-uhd wraistling," he replied, trying to imitate my Louisville accent (badly).

"Hey, Yankee, them's fightin' words!" I said, throwing my helmet down. I went into a boxing stance and gave him a light punch to his shoulder.

Smiling, Austin countered with a round-house punch that barely landed on my chest. "Go back to your grits and pork rinds!"

I threw Austin a body block, enough to send us both tumbling to the ground in a fit of laughter.

Austin pointed to my shirt. "Who's covered with moooo-uhd now?"

Sure enough, I had landed in a wet patch, and the back of my uniform was a solid, gooey brown. As Austin dissolved into hoots of delight, I could hear a familiar but distant voice saying, "Ew, gross, guys!"

I looked around to see Mary Anne sitting in the stands, smiling at us and shaking her head. I had almost forgotten we were going to walk home together that day.

"Hi!" I called out. "I'll be ready in a minute!"

"Ready in a minute, *dear*!" someone to my right echoed, in a nasal, nerdy voice. I looked over to see King and a bunch of other guys snickering. Before I could answer them, I heard Irv Hirsch say something to the effect of, "Why go to the lockers? Just take a shower at *her* house!"

That did it. I took off after them. They split in all directions, laughing and hollering.

I'd been practicing for the hundred-yard dash, and that came in handy. I ended up riding to the lockers on Irv's back as he yelled out, "Just kidding! Come on, get off!"

I know this all must sound pretty dumb, but hey, that's football practice.

Anyway, I showered and dressed in record time. Then I ran outside, shouting good-bye over my shoulder. Mary Anne was leaning against the stands, waiting and smiling.

Okay, now this is the one time I'll get sentimental. That *smile* absolutely kills me. Mary Anne is pretty to begin with, with long, wavy brown hair and piercing brown eyes — and unlike a lot of the girls I knew in my old school, she hardly ever wears makeup (I prefer the natural look). She's also a great listener and has a terrific sense of humor, and I feel totally relaxed around her. But it was her smile that first made me notice her, and to this day it does the most amazing thing to me. It kind of seeps in chest-high and then spreads through me like some incredible magic potion.

The feeling reminds me of something that happened a long time ago. No, nothing romantic. I was about ten. Our family went on a camping trip in the woods and I managed to get lost. My dad says I was gone about ten minutes, but it felt like hours. I really panicked. The sun was casting long shadows and I thought I saw lions and bears behind every tree. I ran and ran and ran, convinced I'd never be found again. Then I turned into a clearing and suddenly I saw my entire family just sitting there. They all looked at me with these huge smiles on their faces. I never felt so happy in my life. All my tension flew away.

That's the kind of feeling I get when Mary Anne smiles at me.

Well, now you heard it. You can laugh if you want, but it's true. And it is the last corny thing I'll say.

"You guys are so funny," Mary Anne said

8

as we walked around the side of the school. "Like little kids."

"Trust me," I said. "You *wouldn't* want to baby-sit for these guys."

"Oooooh, we see you, Bruno!" someone called from behind us. "You can run but you can't hide!"

"Logan and Mary Anne sitting in a tree, K-I-S-S-I-N-G . . ." came King's foghorn singing voice.

Then someone else let out a loud wolf whistle.

Super-mature, huh? At first I wanted to say something, but I just turned to Mary Anne, shrugged, and smiled. We walked off, hand in hand. That made them laugh and "ooohhh" even more, but I didn't care. Before long we were down the block, heading home.

I live closer to school than Mary Anne does, so my house was our first stop. As Mary Anne walked me to the door, I said, "What are you doing tonight?"

"Well, first I have to study for a *math* test," she said with about as much enthusiasm as if she'd said "eat brussels sprouts," or "clean the bathroom."

"Sounds exciting," I said. "Can't wait to hear the details."

Mary Anne smiled. "Thanks a lot."

Now was the time to ask her on a date, and

I had practiced the right way to do it — not too forceful. "Um, want to go out sometime soon?" (Clever and witty, huh?)

"When?" Mary Anne said.

"Well, whenever you're free."

You should have seen Mary Anne's face. It lit up. "Logan, that's so sweet!"

"What is?"

"You didn't just come out and *tell* me what we were going to do!"

I shrugged. "Well, it's what we talked about — "

"Of course I'd like to go out! I'll check the BSC record book at the meeting this afternoon. I don't think I have a Saturday job. Maybe we can talk later on the phone?"

"Okay, I'll call you," I said.

"All right. 'Bye!"

" 'Bye!"

I watched Mary Anne walk away, then went into my house. "I'm ho-ome!" I called out.

"Hi!" Kerry answered from the kitchen.

"Logan! Logan!" Hunter shouted, running toward the front door. I picked him up and buried my head in his stomach, shaking it back and forth. As usual, that made him laugh hysterically.

When I put him down, he said, "Mom's making chicken and ribs."

Actually, it sounded more like, "Bob's bakig

chickid-ad-ribs." Hunter's always stuffed up. He has allergies to just about everything — dust, mold, pollen, animal hair, wheat, milk, strawberries, seafood, you name it. His bedroom has to be dust-free, so you can imagine what it looks like. Bare walls, no rugs, no clutter. I hate to say it, but it looks more like a hospital room than a typical five-year-old's bedroom. Mary Anne feels sorry for him, but Hunter's a real trooper. He *does* have toys (even though they're downstairs), and he likes his room because it's the only place he can go to feel better.

Hunter has the same curly, blondish hair as I do, but that's where the similarity ends. His features are dark like my dad's. Kerry and I look more like my mom, with blue eyes, smallish noses, and long legs (even though Kerry's hair is much straighter and lighter than mine).

"Chicken and ribs? Yum!" I said. The barbecue aroma was already making my stomach twist into a knot of hunger.

Kerry appeared in the living-room archway and asked, "Logan, can you help me with my math?"

"Sure," I said.

"I'll help, too!" Hunter added.

Hunter's "help" meant sitting on Kerry's bed, counting aloud on his fingers, and making comments. Kerry would ask, "Do I carry a two?" and Hunter would say, "I can carry two grocery bags. I can carry *three* footballs . . ." and so on. It was annoying, but kind of funny.

But when my dad called out, "Come help set up!" we bolted out of that room as if it were on fire.

Why? Because there is *nothing* like a good Kentucky barbecue, and my parents make the best. (Dad does the grilling and Mom makes the sauce from scratch.) It's pig heaven.

Kerry took the tablecloth and napkins, Hunter took the utensils, and I took the plates and cups. We barged out the back door just as the phone rang.

Next thing I knew, my mom was calling out the window, "Logan, it's for you."

"Who is it?" I asked, standing there holding the plates as Kerry centered the tablecloth on the picnic table.

"Kristy Thomas!"

"*Lo*-gan . . ." Kerry said, giving me a mischievous look.

"Cut it out," I retorted. "It's probably a sitting job, that's all." (Kristy's the president of the BSC.)

I put my stuff down on the crooked tablecloth, ran inside, and picked up the receiver. "Hello?"

"It's not," came Kristy's voice through the earpiece.

"Huh?"

"It's not a baby-sitting job," Kristy said. "Not exactly. Can you be at Claudia Kishi's house in twenty minutes for our meeting?"

Kristy, as you can guess, likes to get right to the point. "Whoa, slow down," I said. "What's up?"

"It's a long story," Kristy said. "I'll tell you when you get here. Come on, Logan, it's an emergency."

"Well . . . I guess I can come, but — "

"Great! See you!"

Click. Dial tone. End of conversation.

I hung up the phone feeling completely confused — and a little nervous. Kristy can be somewhat . . . *brusque*, as my mom would say, but I'd never heard her speak like that.

Something was wrong, and I had to know what it was.

CHAPTER 2

"Everything okay, Logan?" my mom asked.

"Uh, yeah," I answered. "I think — "

My dad was lifting a platter of neatly stacked, sauce-drenched, raw chicken parts off the kitchen table. "Want to give me a hand at the grill?" he asked.

"Well, I just told Kristy I'd go to a BSC meeting. It'll only last till six. She says it's an emergency."

"Emergency?" Dad repeated, looking a little skeptical.

"Yeah," I said. "Kristy didn't say what it was."

"Go ahead, honey," Mom said. "We won't eat before then."

We both looked at the stove clock. It was after five.

"I don't know, Logan," Dad said. "The ribs might be gone by then."

I held the back door open for him. "Better not be!" I said with a smile.

Dad shrugged. "You're taking your chances."

I laughed, then ran to the garage, yelling, " 'Bye!"

" 'Bye!" Kerry and Hunter called back.

I pulled my bike out of the garage and tore off down the driveway.

Did you notice my dad's reaction? Not negative, but a little . . . uncomfortable. He gets that way when I mention anything to do with the BSC. He's not a real macho-type, just old-fashioned. For example, he'll talk to me for hours about so-and-so's batting average, or the best way to run a defense against a strong quarterback, anything related to sports. (Which makes sense when you consider he's a manager for a sporting-goods manufacturer.) But when I mention some funny or interesting thing that happened during a sitting job, he puts on this little, tolerant smile, and just nods silently.

In his mind, I'm only involved in the BSC because I'm hot for Mary Anne, and *that* makes it okay.

(Well, in a way, he's right.)

Just in a way, though. I do enjoy kids, and I also like the other club members. Kristy, Stacey, Claudia, Dawn, Mal, and Jessi are among my best friends — even though they're girls. I know that "even though" part may sound stupid, but some guys think girls are a form of human asparagus. You know, keep away at all costs.

Let's face it, I can't *do* the same things with them that I do with Austin or Trevor Sandbourne, or any of my guy friends. With guys I can be freer. We wrestle, say insulting things without being taken seriously, stuff like that. But you know what? Sometimes I actually prefer being around girls. You can talk about how you're feeling without being made to feel dorky. Girls actually listen and try to understand, instead of yawn and change the subject. Also, to be blunt about it, girls are nicer to look at.

(I can't help saying that. They *are*!)

Now that I've mentioned their names, let me tell you about the BSC members. I'll start with the one I know best, Mary Anne Spier.

Don't worry. I'm not going to repeat what I said about her smile and the day I got lost in the woods and all that. There are quite a few other things I didn't mention. Like the fact that her mom died when she was little, so she was raised by her dad. His name is Richard, but I would never dream of calling him anything but Mr. Spier. He's a nice guy, but not exactly Mr. Laid Back. If you've ever seen reruns of that show, *The Odd Couple*, he's like Felix, the neat one. Everything *has* to be just so. What was it like growing up with him? Not easy, according to Mary Anne. He made her dress in little-girl clothes and wear her hair in pigtails right up till seventh grade. There were rules about *everything* — phone calls, friends, staying out late, homework, TV, makeup.

When I feel like complaining about my parents, all I have to do is think about what Mary Anne went through.

Yes, I did say *went*, past tense. Mary Anne looks and dresses her age now. Felix — I mean, Mr. Spier — has changed a lot. Why? Well, if you ask Dawn Schafer, marriage did it to him (*re*marriage, to be exact). You see, Mr. Spier married Dawn's mother.

Before I go into that, let me tell you about Dawn. She's another BSC member, and she's as different from Mary Anne as . . . well, as Mr. Spier is from Mrs. Schafer. Dawn is a blonde with a capital *B*. Not sandy blonde or dirty blonde or strawberry blonde, but *blonde* blonde. She's funny and full of energy and *very* individualistic. For example, she eats nothing but health food. No meats, no sweets. She would starve at one of my family barbecues, unless we could figure out a way to charbroil a hunk of tofu.

17

Dawn lived in California till seventh grade, when her parents divorced. Mrs. Schafer happens to be a Stoneybrook native, and she decided to bring her kids back here to live (Dawn has a ten-year-old brother, Jeff). They moved into this spooky old farmhouse that was built in the 1700s. Dawn says it has a secret passage that leads from her bedroom to the barn, probably left over from the days when the house was a stop on the Underground Railroad.

So there they were, a family of three rattling around in that house. But before long, Jeff got homesick for California (and for his dad) and was allowed to move back. This was a sad and lonely time for Dawn. Then Mrs. Schafer, who's pretty and young-seeming and disorganized, fell in love with . . . Felix! I should say, they fell *back* in love. It seems they were high school sweethearts long ago.

Well, they married, and Mary Anne and her dad moved into the farmhouse. The family of two became four, and Dawn and Mary Anne, who were already best friends, became stepsisters, too.

Mary Anne's other best friend is the famous Kristy Thomas, the only other girl who could tear me away from a Bruno family barbecue. Kristy's a born leader, a terrific athlete, and a real "idea" person. A lot of people find her loud and bossy, but I think that's because her mind works so fast that she gets frustrated with people who think at normal speed. She was the one who thought of the Baby-sitters Club, and she's a big reason it's doing so well (details later). It would take me forever to describe some of the things she thought of, but my favorite example is Kristy's Krushers. That's the name of a softball team she formed, made up of kids who aren't ready to play in Little League. She managed to get them uniforms, equipment, the works.

Kristy looks a little like Mary Anne. They both have brown, shoulder-length hair and dark eyes, but Kristy's shorter and not as clothes-conscious. Now, Mary Anne is not exactly into high fashion, but to Kristy, anything besides jeans and a turtleneck is dressing up.

If you thought Mary Anne's family situation was unusual, wait till I tell you about Kristy's. It started out relatively normal: a mom, a dad, two older brothers (Charlie and Sam), and a younger brother named David Michael. Then, not long after David Michael was born (Kristy was only six), Mr. Thomas just up and left. No one knows why, and Kristy doesn't like to talk about it. Suddenly Mrs. Thomas had to get a full-time job and raise a family of four on her own — which she did, somehow.

Then along came Watson Brewer, Knight in

Shining Armor. Actually, he wasn't a Sir Lancelot type (unless Lancelot was quiet and balding and liked gardening), but Mrs. Thomas fell in love with him. He happened to be a millionaire who lived in a real mansion on the other side of town.

Soon Kristy had a stepfather, and the Thomas family was moving into that mansion!

Watson has two kids from a previous marriage, who come to live with him every other weekend. (Karen's seven and Andrew's four.) The mansion had been a pretty lonely place for him — but not any more. After Kristy's family moved in, Watson and Mrs. Thomas adopted a Vietnamese girl and named her Emily Michelle. (She's almost three.) To help take care of her, Kristy's grandmother also moved in. Throw in a puppy, a grouchy old cat, and two goldfish, and you have a pretty full house, even for a mansion.

Now, on to Claudia Kishi, who has a small, manageable family. Well, maybe not so manageable. Claud's had her share of trouble dealing with her sister Janine, who has an IQ that makes teachers drool. Claudia used to feel incredibly inferior and thought her parents were playing favorites with Janine. But even though Claudia's just an average student, she's an amazing artist, and the rest of her family has begun respecting that. It's about time, too, because Claud can draw, paint, sculpt, make jewelry and clothing . . .

And *eat*. That's her other main talent. She's a junk-food maniac. I think she could survive on Ring Dings and Snickers bars for weeks and never complain. You'd expect someone like that to have weight trouble, right? Guess again. Claudia looks like a model. She's really slim, with long, jet-black hair. Her skin is perfect, and she has these gorgeous, almond-shaped eyes. (Her family's Japanese-American.) She also has a really hip, sexy way of dressing.

Okay, time out. Let me say right here that I am just *describing*. Mary Anne is my girl-friend, but that doesn't mean I can't say positive things about someone else's looks.

All right. That's all I wanted to say. Didn't want you to worry.

Keeping that in mind, let me move on to Stacey McGill. She's the BSC's only New Yorker. She ended up in Stoneybrook when her dad got a job here. Then her dad was transferred back to New York and she had to leave the BSC. Next thing everyone knew, she was back again, this time with only her mother. Her parents had divorced. It must have been a tough time for her, but at least she had some great friends to come back to.

Stacey is tall, blonde, and pretty. She

dresses great, like Claudia, except her clothes are maybe less wild and more sophisticated. In fact, sophisticated is a perfect word to describe Stacey. Not *snobby* sophisticated, but smart and witty and mature. In a way, I think Stacey had to grow up faster than most people I know. Not just because of the divorce, either. You see, she has this condition called diabetes, which means her body can't regulate the amount of sugar in her blood. She has to give herself daily injections of insulin. And if she missed one, she could get really sick. *I* would grow up pretty fast if I had to deal with something like that.

The BSC has two younger members, Jessi Ramsey and Mallory Pike. They're sixth-graders and *excellent* sitters, both very level-headed and great with kids. Jessi is the BSC's only black member. In fact, the Ramseys are one of the few black families in Stoneybrook. And let me tell you, it was *not* easy for them when they first moved in. A few people got really uptight and made it hard for the Ramseys — you know, racial comments and suspicious stares and your basic stupid prejudice. What made it especially hard was that the Ramseys had moved from a racially mixed town where everyone got along fine. Fortunately, things became better in Stoneybrook for Jessi and her family, and they seem pretty happy now.

Jessi's the oldest of the Ramsey kids. Her sister, Becca, is eight, and her brother, Squirt (short for John Philip), is about a year and a half.

I should mention that Jessi is a future star ballerina. She takes lessons twice a week, and practices at home all the time. She *looks* like a dancer, too, with long, thin legs and pulled-back hair.

Mallory is white, and she has curly hair, freckles, and glasses. She's Jessi's best friend, and it's easy to see why. They both love reading books about horses, they both complain that their parents treat them like babies, they're both the oldest kid in their families (except Mal has *seven* brothers and sisters), and they're both really creative. Mal's special talent is writing and illustrating. She's always making up children's stories, which is what she wants to do professionally someday.

And that's it for the regular BSC members. Then there are the irregulars — me and Shannon Kilbourne, the two associate members. Shannon lives in Kristy's neighborhood and goes to a private school called Stoneybrook Day School. Neither of us is required to attend meetings, but we do get a fair amount of work.

For me, meetings are not especially comfortable. I like everybody, but being the only guy in a room full of girls is a little weird, especially if they're all good friends. No one is totally at ease.

So I felt a little nervous as I hopped on my bike and headed to the meeting — normal nervousness plus nervousness about what the "emergency" was. I hoped it was worth being late for a barbecue.

CHAPTER 3

Hot dogs.

Spare ribs.

Corn on the cob.

And sausage, I think.

Those were the smells drifting out of people's backyards as I pedaled toward Claudia Kishi's house. I noticed every one. *Man*, I must have been hungry.

Oh, well. I knew within minutes I'd be eating *something*, even if it was only chips or chocolate or popcorn or something else delicious and not good for you.

That's what happens when your club meets at the house of the world's number one junk-food addict. (One thing I didn't mention about Claudia is that she is *very* generous with her supply.)

Maybe I should tell you a little about the BSC and its high-calorie meetings. First of all, Claudia's room is headquarters because she's the only member with her own phone line. Her number is also the BSC's official number.

Here's how the club works. Every Monday, Wednesday, and Friday, the main members meet in Claud's room at 5:30 *sharp* (Kristy makes sure of that). From then until 6:00, the club takes calls from parents who need sitters. Since there are seven members (nine including Shannon and me), someone is usually available. Great idea, huh? Parents don't have to go calling individual sitters all over town, and BSC members can count on some pretty steady work.

How do parents know about the BSC? Nowadays it's mostly word-of-mouth. Satisfied clients are the best advertising, because they often refer their friends to us. Way back when the club was starting, members used to put posters and fliers in supermarkets, day care centers, and pediatricians' offices. We still do that from time to time, if business is slow.

Actually, the BSC *is* a business in many ways, complete with officers. Claudia, for example, is the vice-president. She doesn't really have formal duties, but she provides the room, the phone, and snacks, so it's only right she should have a title.

Kristy, as I said before, is the president. She's a *born* president — firm and fair and overflowing with ideas. A little overbearing sometimes, but nobody's perfect. I wouldn't be surprised to see her in the White House someday. Or at least at the head of a company.

Kristy was the one who thought up the BSC. It happened back before her mom had met Sir Lancelot . . . I mean, Watson. One afternoon Mrs. Thomas needed a sitter for David Michael, so she got out her list. She called every sitter, one by one, and each was busy or not home. By the tenth call or so, she was getting frazzled, and Kristy's mind was hard at work. If only there were some sort of central number for baby-sitters, like a switchboard. . . . All at once lightning flashed, the clouds parted, the sun came streaming through. Okay, I'm exaggerating, but Kristy did think of the Baby-sitters Club in that moment. She called Mary Anne and Claudia (the three original members), and the club was born. Stacey joined, then Dawn, and eventually Shannon and me. When Stacey moved to New York, Jessi and Mallory became members — and they stayed on when Stacey came back.

Since then, Kristy's been the club's unofficial Idea Person. She gets ideas all the time, and no matter how crazy they seem, she manages to pull them off. One example was Kristy's Krushers, which I already mentioned. She also thinks of special holiday events, play groups, and craft projects. But some of her best ideas are her simplest, like Kid-Kits. Those are decorated boxes full of old games and toys, drawing supplies, and so on, that we bring along on sitting jobs. It's all secondhand stuff, but kids *love* Kid-Kits.

Oh, here's another Kristy idea: the BSC notebook. We're supposed to write in it about our sitting jobs — tips about any new clients, news about our charges' likes and dislikes, funny or unusual experiences, stuff like that. It's very useful, even though everyone complains about having to write in it.

If Kristy's the Idea Person, Mary Anne's the Organization Person. As club secretary, she's in charge of the BSC record book. It's the hardest job, no question. And I'm not just saying that because she's my girlfriend. First of all, she oversees the appointment calendar. Whenever a call comes in, Mary Anne checks to see who's available, which means keeping track of everyone's conflicts, like after-school activities, doctor appointments, and family trips. Then she has to consider whether the sitting jobs are spread evenly around. In the back of the book, she keeps an up-to-date list of all client addresses and phone numbers.

I'd go crazy if I had to do her job, but Mary Anne laughs whenever I say that. To her, it's second nature. Piece of cake.

If the Baby-sitters Club were a baseball team,

Kristy would be the manager and Mary Anne would be the team statistician. Claudia would design the stadium *and* the uniforms.

And Stacey would sign the checks. She's the club treasurer, which is fitting, because she's a math whiz. On Mondays she collects club dues from everyone (except Shannon and me, lucky us), which she uses to cover monthly club expenses. Charlie Thomas is paid for driving Kristy to meetings, and Claudia is given money to help with her phone bill. Sometimes Kid-Kits need to be replenished, or somebody has to be paid back for photocopying flyers, and other things like that. Then, if anything is left over, the club sometimes has a pizza party (yeah!) or a sleepover (boo!).

Dawn is our alternate officer, which means she can substitute for anyone in an emergency. I think she's done each job at least once. When Stacey moved to New York, Dawn filled in as treasurer the whole time (and gave the job back gladly when Stacey returned).

Mal and Jessi are the junior officers, which is a polite way of saying they're the two youngest. Their parents don't like them to stay out late, so they take a lot of the afternoon and weekend jobs. That really helps, because it frees everyone else for nighttime sitting.

And that's the lineup, as Coach Mills would say.

By the time I parked my bike at the side of Claudia's house, my mouth felt dry. Would this be like the last meeting I went to, where the girls kept looking at each other whenever I said anything, and half of them seemed to want to laugh? I hoped not. It's easier to face a line of scrimmage than that.

I walked to the front door. Janine must have seen me coming, because she opened the door. "They're upstairs," she said. She sounded solemn, but I figured that was just Janine.

I smiled. "Thanks."

Janine adjusted her glasses and walked into the kitchen.

I took the stairs two at a time. Something was bugging me. No sound was coming from Claudia's room. At the last meeting I went to, you could practically hear the giggling and gabbing from the street.

When I reached the upstairs hallway, I could hear very soft talking. Then there was a gasp or a gulp or something.

Claudia's door was shut, so I knocked softly. She opened it. I was a little shocked by her serious expression.

"Claudia, what's wrong?" I blurted out.

That's when she swung the door open all the way, and I saw tears streaming down Mary Anne's face.

30

CHAPTER 4

"Hi, Logan," Kristy said in a grave voice. "Sit."

I seated myself on the bed and put my arm around Mary Anne. "Hey, are you all right?" I asked.

Mary Anne nodded and tried to smile. The smile lasted about a thousandth of a second, and she buried her face in my shoulder. I held onto her and looked around. Kristy was sitting in the director's chair by Claudia's desk. Her eyebrows were knitted together, making a ledge over her eyes.

Jessi and Mal were sitting on the floor, crosslegged and heads down, both fiddling with the carpet.

Stacey was pacing, deep in thought about something.

Claudia was sitting next to us, without any food in her hand. That made me worry almost

31

as much as Mary Anne's crying did.

I realized someone was missing. "Where's Dawn?" I asked.

Kristy lowered her head and sighed. She looked at Mary Anne. "Do you want me to tell him?"

Mary Anne nodded.

My stomach went into a knot. I thought . . . well, I don't even want to tell you what I thought. This meeting was giving me the creeps.

Kristy took a deep breath. "First of all, Dawn is all right, so don't worry," she said. "But she *is* pretty shook up. It looks like she and her mom have to go to California."

"You mean, for good?" I asked.

"Oh, no," Kristy replied. "I guess I better start from the beginning. When Mary Anne got home this afternoon, her dad was there, talking on the kitchen phone, which was a little weird, because he's usually not home by then. Mary Anne figured there'd been a plumbing emergency or something, and he was calling a repair shop. So she went upstairs to change, and that's when she heard Dawn and Mrs. Schafer."

She paused. I was dying for her to get to the point, but in case you didn't notice, Kristy likes to be dramatic.

"They were both crying and packing suitcases," she went on. "So Mary Anne ran into Dawn's room and asked what was wrong. Well, Dawn was so upset she could hardly talk. It seems her mom had gotten a frantic call at work from her dad in California. Jeff had to be rushed to the hospital today with a ruptured appendix."

So that's what it was. Mary Anne was upset because her stepsister was so upset. I hugged her tighter. "That's terrible," I said.

Kristy nodded sagely. "We were just saying how Stacey's uncle had had a ruptured appendix, and he almost died."

Just the right thing to bring up. Mary Anne began shaking. "Kristy . . ." I said.

"It's all right," Mary Anne said softly. "The doctors said he'll be okay. But it's going to take him a few weeks to recover from the operation."

"Anyway, Dawn and her mom are going to go to California to be with him till he's better," Kristy said. She sighed, tapping a pencil on her lap. "So . . . Dawn's not going to be around for a couple of weeks."

"I'm sure everything will be fine," I said to Mary Anne. But when I looked up, I could see that everyone was staring at me.

Suddenly a question popped into my head. Why exactly had I been invited to this meeting? To comfort Mary Anne, sure. But she didn't really *need* me for that. "Um, is there something I can do?" I asked.

"Uh, yeah," Kristy said. "Dawn had some jobs scheduled. A lot, really. It's going to be hard to shuffle around the rest of us . . ."

"I can take some of them," I said confidently. "No problem."

"That's great," Kristy said. "That'll really help. But the actual reason we asked you to the meeting was . . . well, we were wondering if you could take Dawn's place, Logan. Just while she's gone."

Uh-oh.

"You mean, do *all* her jobs?" I asked.

"Not all," Claudia spoke up. "We can split them up."

"What I mean is, take her place at the meetings," Kristy said. "Be here when the jobs come in. Be our alternate officer — "

"We're really swamped," Stacey cut in. "A bunch of new clients have called. Losing even one member is going to be, like, insane for us."

"We asked Shannon," Claudia said, "but she has too many commitments."

Too many commitments? I thought. More than football practice, and training for the track team? "Well, um, I'm not sure I can . . ."

"It's just a few meetings, Logan," Mary

Anne said. "Practice ends early enough, and we can make sure there's some snack food here if you're hungry."

"The meetings, sure," I said. "But so many *jobs* are right after school, just when practice starts."

"You might not have to take those jobs," Stacey said.

"If you did, would you be able to miss a practice?" Mary Anne asked. "I mean, does everyone go to every practice?"

"Well, no," I said. "People do miss practice sometimes, in an emergency."

"I think this counts as an emergency, and you *are* a member of the BSC," Kristy pointed out. "Look, I know it's not fair to pressure you, Logan. But if you can't do it, let us know, because we'll have to find someone brand new to train."

I drew in a deep breath. It was hard to say no when everyone was counting on me. And I had to admit, I probably could work this into my schedule. It would be tough, but I could do it.

"Okay," I said with a nod. "We're in business."

"Yea!" Mary Anne cried out, squeezing me tightly.

Jessi and Mal grinned at me, and Stacey said, "I knew he'd say yes!"

Kristy was beaming. "Thanks, Logan. You really saved us."

Claudia reached under her pillow and pulled out a box of chocolate marshmallow cookies. "Celebration!" she said. She passed them to her right, then fished a bag of tortilla chips from underneath her bed. "For the health-food crowd," she said, handing the bag to Stacey.

Kristy had already shifted into her presidential mode. It was 5:37, and she *hates* to do anything late. "Hrrmph. I call our regular meeting to order!"

"Monday . . . dues day!" Stacey chirped.

Grumble, grumble, grumble, everyone else replied. But they dug out their money and handed it over.

"Not you, Logan," Stacey said as I reached into my pocket. "You're doing us enough of a favor."

"Lucky," Claudia murmured.

Everyone laughed a little, then talked a little, and then . . .

Silence.

No, not exactly. There were some crunching sounds, and the crackling of plastic. There were also a lot of shifting of eyes and looking at the phone.

In other words, it was just like the last meeting I went to. Suddenly I didn't know if I'd made the right choice.

"Uh, is it something I said?" I asked.

Nothing like a dumb joke to break the ice. They all burst into giggles. Finally Stacey said, "Come on, guys! Loosen up a little. Just 'cause there's a *guy* in here — "

"He's not a *guy*!" Mary Anne protested. "He's Logan!"

More laughs.

"Oops," Mary Anne said as I shot her a Look. I was about to reply, but that was when the phone rang for the first time.

Claudia snatched up the receiver and said, "Hello, Baby-sitters Club!" It was Mrs. Prezzioso, one of our regular clients. Claudia took the information, Mary Anne flipped through the record book, and the meeting was in full gear.

For the first time, I could sit back and think.

And I was sorry I did. My mind filled up with questions. What if I did have to miss practice? What would I tell the coach, "I have a baby-sitting job"? What would he say to that? And what about the other guys? I could just imagine Irv Hirsch's reaction, and Clarence King's.

Then there was my *track* tryout. I'd been practicing my sprints after football. I'd miss some practice — and boy, did I need it.

So here's what the BSC was going to mean: letting down the coach, opening myself to ridicule, and getting rejected from track.

Some sacrifice!

"Logan?" I heard Mary Anne say. "Are you okay?"

"Sure," I replied.

Okay, I lied. But after all, a commitment is a commitment.

"Ooooh!" Kristy exclaimed. "Did you guys read about that health fair at the shopping center?"

"I think I saw a poster." Mal replied.

"It sounds interesting," Kristy said. "They're going to have all these booths — you know, health-related stuff. Like how to eat and exercise right, how to do first aid, safety tips around the house. I think they're going to have a bloodmobile, too."

"Yuck," Claudia said. "I went to one of those once. They checked my blood pressure and told me to eat seaweed and oat bran."

"Are you going to donate someday?" Stacey asked.

" Maybe when I have a paying job," Claudia said.

Stacey rolled her eyes. "No, I mean *blood*. You can start donating when you're seventeen, I think."

"Ew! Are you kidding?" Claudia replied with a shudder.

"What blood type are you?" Stacey insisted.

Claudia shrugged. "I don't know. O, I think my dad once told me."

"The universal donor," Stacey replied. "You *should* give blood. What would happen if I passed out from insulin shock, broke open my head, and needed a transfusion?"

"Stacey, that's gross!" Claudia exclaimed.

"Well, it could happen. And there's a shortage of donor blood in this country. What if they just happened to need a pint of O blood for me?"

"Okay, okay, the *minute* I turn seventeen I'll sign up," Claudia said. "But one of you will have to be there to clean up my barf."

To a chorus of "ews" and embarrassed laughter, Stacey said, "*Now* who's being gross?"

"I think Kristy's right," I spoke up. The fair made me think of Hunter, and how conscious my family had to be of his health. "We should go to the fair."

"Actually," Kristy said, "I thought we could set up a booth ourselves."

"Huh?" Mallory reached for a chocolate marshmallow cookie. "For what? Junk food management?"

"No," Kristy said. "Something related to baby-sitting."

"What does that have to do with health?" Mary Anne asked.

"I don't know," replied Kristy (using three words I hardly ever hear come out of her mouth). "We could figure out *something*. The point is, it would be great publicity for us."

"But you just can't walk right in and set up a booth," Claudia remarked. "Can you?"

"The poster listed a phone number for the booth chairperson," Kristy answered. "I'll call and ask. If she says yes, we'll think of a theme."

We talked about it a little more. To tell you the truth, I was happy to get my mind off my dilemma. In fact, I forgot about the dilemma until the phone rang at about five to six.

"Hello, Baby-sitters Club!" Claudia said. "Hi, Mr. Hobart . . . Fine, thanks . . . This Thursday, after school till seven? OK, I'll call you back." She hung up the phone and glanced at Mary Anne.

Mary Anne's face was buried in the record book. "Just a minute, this is confusing. Dawn was going to sit for the Barretts, and Claudia said she'd cover that . . . Jessi has a class . . . Mal and Stacey are at the Pikes' . . . Kristy's at the Papadakises' . . . That's my day for Rosie Wilder . . ."

She looked up at me with this funny expression, half apologetic and half pitying. "That leaves you, Logan."

Cheerful thoughts of the health fair fizzled away. Two things sank in: One, I was now officially a full member of the Baby-sitters Club. And two, I was going to miss my first football practice. Ever.

I knew it was going to be a long two weeks.

CHAPTER 5

"First I'm going to shoot the bear with my bow and arrow. Then I'm going to chop off his head and skin him and put him in the oven and eat him."

Johnny Hobart was having a life crisis. In the last few weeks, he had decided that everyone around was bigger than he was, smarter than he was, and stronger than he was. And he had come to the conclusion that there was only one thing to do about it.

Kill them all.

Johnny is four years old. I wondered if I was like that when I was his age. If I was, I can't believe my parents didn't send me packing.

"Johnny," said his older brother Mathew. "We're *camping*, remember? Not hunting!"

Johnny dropped his imaginary bow. "Oh, right."

Ow, roit, is how it came out. Yes, there are other people in Stoneybrook who speak with accents. The Hobarts are from Australia, and their accent is sort of like British, with a twang.

You can see why I like them so much.

Anyway, there are four Hobart brothers. But Ben and James (who are twelve and eight) were clothes shopping with their mother, so I was sitting for the younger two.

As Mathew had said, we were setting up camp. We had collected tent gear, pots, pans, silverware, backpacks loaded with provisions, and sleeping bags. We were going to learn about survival in the outdoors, dealing with the elements, fighting off bears and wolves, and rationing food and water.

And we were going to do it all on the Hobarts' front lawn.

"Camping out" was a game some of Mathew's friends had told him about. Mathew had never played it himself, but he was dying to. And I thought it seemed like a perfect activity for a sitting job.

"Here," Johnny said, taking a coonskin cap off his head. "Wear this. It's making my hair sweat."

The "fur" was fake and looked terrible, and the cap was warm and clammy and way too small for me. It had a ratty-looking tail, like someone had been plucking it. But hey, part of being a sitter is being able to make a fool of yourself when necessary, right? So I

perched the cap on my head and sang, "Davy
. . . Davy Crockett!"

"Come on, mate!" Mathew called out as he
dragged an old sheet across the lawn. "We
have to pitch this tent before sunset." He
dropped the sheet, stood in a sunny spot, and
pointed to his shadow. "See how late it is!"

"How late?" Johnny asked.

Mathew licked his finger and held it in the
air. "Eleven-seventeen!"

I managed not to laugh. Mathew, by the
way, is six. And of course, he's much, much
smarter and more mature than his little
brother.

According to Mathew.

He and Johnny tried to drape the old sheet
over a couple of sawhorses I'd dragged out of
the garage. I helped them center the sheet,
then we cut some twine and tied each corner
to stout, pointy twigs we'd found. Using a
rock, we drove our "stakes" into the ground
and anchored our tent.

"Yea!" Johnny cried out. "Now we can hide
in here from the bear!"

Mathew shook his head with an I-can't-
believe-how-dumb-he-is expression. "No,
silly," he said. "He'll see right through. *I'll*
show you what we have to do."

He climbed the stairs to the Hobarts' porch

and lifted a webbed lawn chair. "You guys bring some down, too!"

We followed his command, and soon four chairs stood in a semicircle in front of the tent. "There," Mathew said.

"Uh . . . why *four* chairs, Mathew?" I asked.

"One for the bear." Mathew said. "See, we'll leave out food for him to eat. Then he won't hate us, so he'll sit down and we can come out and talk to him."

"What are we going to feed him?" Johnny asked.

Mathew reached into his backpack and pulled out a rattly box of cookies. "Teddy Grahams!" he announced.

That did make me laugh. "I think if you gave him bears to eat, he might get mad."

"Yeah!" Johnny squealed. "And then I'll shoot him!"

"Okay, guys, here's a question," I said. "If you think there are bears near your campsite, where's the best place to keep your food safe?"

"Under a blanket?" Mathew suggested.

I shook my head. "He would smell it there."

Johnny piped up, "Then I would eat the food real fast, and take a gun, and — "

"Shoot him," Mathew interrupted. "We know. We heard you a million times."

"Here's a hint," I said. "Put it someplace

where the bear can't get it." I gave a not-too-subtle look straight up to an overhanging branch.

"Hang it from a tree!" Mathew blurted out.

"Right!" I replied. "Come on, let's do it. If it's already eleven-seventeen, it's past bedtime, and bears come out at night."

With a long piece of twine, we tied up the packs and flung them over the branch. (The packs were mostly filled with cookies and granola, so they weren't very heavy.) To anchor them, I tied the loose end of the twine around a heavy rock.

"Hey, what if he just pulls this end of the rope?" Mathew asked, pointing to the part that was tied to the rock.

"Well, we'll see if he's smart enough," I said. "Johnny, you be the bear, and Mathew and I will be sleeping campers."

Johnny's eyes lit up. "Okay!"

Mathew and I scurried under the sawhorses. We started making snoring noises.

"Ooooh, ooooh, ooooh," came Johnny's voice.

"Those are *monkey* noises!" Mathew called out. "Bears *growl*!"

"Oh," Johnny said. Then, a few seconds later, "Grrrrrrr, rrrrrrrr!"

"Aaaaaaah!" Mathew yelled, scrambling out of the tent.

I put on my trusty coonskin cap and followed him. Johnny was stomping around angrily, his face twisted into a snarl. We ran away, and he lumbered after us. When we reached the other side of the yard, he stopped. "Yummmm," he murmured, looking up at the hanging backpacks.

As Johnny began pulling at the twine, Mathew cried out, "Get away from there!" He ran to the tent, picked up a pot, and held it threateningly over his head. "That's *our* food, bear!"

"Mathew, stop!" Johnny protested. "I'm going to tell Mom!"

Oops. Our campground was about to become a battleground. I had to think fast.

"Hey!" I yelled, grabbing a frying pan. "Look what's coming!"

"What?" both boys asked.

I pointed to the dogwood tree by the side of the house. "It's a saber-toothed wildcat, the greatest enemy of people and bears!"

"I'll scratch him with my claws!" Johnny said.

"I'll bash him!" Mathew cried out, clutching his pot.

"Okay, stick together, guys. Shoulder to shoulder!" I said. They ran to my sides. I adjusted my coonskin cap, pushing it low over my eyes. "Let's get him!"

The three of us rushed toward the dogwood, yelling like crazy. Mathew and I flailed at the imaginary attacker with our pot and pan, and Johnny swiped with his "claws."

And that was when I heard the laughter behind us.

I turned to look. The tail of the coonskin cap swished across my face. In front of the house, straddling their bikes, were King, Pete Black, Jim Poirier, and Irv Hirsch — all members of the football team. Their hair was slicked down from post-practice showers, their backpacks sagged with the weight of sweaty gym clothes.

"Nice hat," Pete called out.

I yanked off the cap, but it was too late. The four of them were pointing at me and whooping with hysterical laughter.

"Come on, Logan," Mathew said, uncertainly.

I felt my face growing hot. It must have been as red as raw hamburger. My mind went blank. I said something like, "Hey, guys, how was practice?"

"Fine, Wogan," Jim said, in a baby voice. "We pwayed wif the big baw and then took a nappie."

Well, they practically fell off their bikes at that. Part of me wanted to laugh along with them, but I couldn't. Johnny and Mathew were just standing there, looking hurt and confused, and they were my responsibility.

I walked up to the guys, trying to act as cool as possible under the circumstances. "Look, guys, this was an emergency job I had to do for some . . . friends."

"Who, the *Baby-sitters Club*?" King asked sarcastically.

"Yeah, well, you know, my girlfriend is a member," I said.

"That's why he missed practice?" Pete asked, with this look of total disbelief.

"Uh-huh." King hopped onto his bike seat. "Come on, guys. Logan's too busy to talk to us."

"Do we have to go?" Jim whined, sticking out his lower lip. "I wanted to pway wif dem!"

" 'Bye, Bwuno!" Irv squealed.

They pedaled away, howling with laughter.

I looked down at the grass and exhaled. Wow, did I feel like a dork. Not to mention a liar, I hadn't told them I was a *member* of the BSC. Plus I'd let down Johnny and Mathew by not sticking up for them. And then there was the hat.

Good work, Bruno.

I felt someone tugging at my sleeve. "Logan?"

It was Mathew. "Are we going to finish fighting the wildcat?"

"Yeah," I said. "Sure."

Johnny was holding the coonskin cap out to me. "Here."

"Thanks," I said. "Okay, go get him! He's attacking the tent!"

The brothers yelped happily and ran toward the tent, ready for battle.

While their backs were turned, I let the coonskin cap fall to the ground, then followed behind them. I wasn't going to take any chances.

We played a little while longer, and then began "breaking camp." As we cleaned up, Mrs. Hobart turned into the driveway and beeped her horn. Ben Hobart waved to us from the passenger seat.

"Mommy! Ben!" Johnny and Mathew yelled. "Look at our tent!"

Mrs. Hobart was smiling broadly as she slid out of the car and walked across the lawn. "Well, it looks as if I have a house full of happy campers!" she said cheerily.

I smiled back. She was right about two of us.

"Hello, Baby-sitters Club!"

Only fifteen minutes into our Friday BSC meeting, the day after the Hobart disaster, and Claudia was taking our fourth call.

So far I'd been lucky, in two ways. First of all, there was no football practice that afternoon, so I didn't have to show my face to King and the other guys. Second, I'd managed to avoid having to take any of the day's sitting offers.

"Oh, hi, Mrs. Hobart!" Claudia continued.

I had a feeling my luck was about to change.

"Uh-huh . . . Sure, I'll ask him. Can I call you back in a second? . . . Thanks . . . 'bye."

She hung up and gave me a shrug. "The boys are in love with you, Logan. They want you to sit for them Monday and a week from Saturday. I didn't want to say yes, because I thought you might have practice."

"Well, practice is Tuesday and Thursday next week," I said. "So I guess it's all right."

51

"Great," Claudia said, grabbing the phone again.

That was how I got my second and third sitting jobs. The fourth one came about ten minutes later, a Tuesday job at the Rodowskys'.

Yes, Tuesday. I was going to miss my second football practice in a row. And since I often stayed late to practice for track tryouts, I was going to miss that, too.

But you know what? I wasn't going to let any of this get me down. I couldn't salvage the football practice, but I vowed to go to the track on Saturday and work out.

The minute I made that promise to myself, I felt much better. I sat back, relaxed, and decided to make the best of it.

And that was when Kristy brought up her latest great idea again. "Oh! You guys, I forgot to mention I called the health fair chairperson. Her name's Ms. Bernstein, and she's really nice. And she was *thrilled* we want to set up a booth. But she needs to know what we're going to do, so she can include the information in the poster for the fair."

"It should be pretty easy to figure *something* out," Stacey said.

"Let's see, health ideas . . ." Claudia said, biting into a Twinkie.

"How about contacting people from a couple of health professions?" Jessi suggested. "We could ask Dr. Johanssen to come and talk to kids—"

"There'll by plenty of doctors and nurses there," Kristy interrupted.

"I know!" Stacey said. "What about nutrition for kids?"

"Yeah, the four basic food groups and stuff like that," Claudia agreed.

"What *are* the four basic food groups?" asked Mal.

Claud put down her half-eaten Twinkie. "Fruits," she began, counting confidently on her fingers, "vegetables, starches, and . . . um, candy, I think."

Everyone giggled. (I, of course, being a guy, laughed.)

"We could raffle off some health food," Mary Anne said.

"And what would the winners get?" Jessi asked.

"A week's worth of soy burgers," Claudia suggested.

"We have to do something practical," Kristy said, "something we know about."

Then I had an idea. "How about *safe* sitting?" I said. "That has to do with health, in a way. We could give out information on baby-sitting techniques, like how to deal with a kid who starts choking on food."

"We could demonstrate the Heimlich maneuver!" Mal said.

"Or suggest helpful tips," Stacey added, "like never leave a baby alone while he's taking a bath, even if there are only a couple of inches of water in the tub."

"That's a great idea!" Kristy said. "We could put it all in a pamphlet and distribute the pamphlets — with a BSC flier attached!"

"Would they allow that?" Stacey wondered. "Advertising, I mean."

"I'll ask," Kristy replied. "In the meantime, let's list the things we're going to put in the pamphlet."

Mary Anne opened the record book to a blank pad in the back. "Okay, shoot."

"Always keep one hand on a baby when she's on a changing table," Jessi suggested.

"Make sure to get the phone number of the restaurant or theater your client is going to," Stacey said.

"Check all electrical sockets to see if they're covered," Mal said.

"Always know where there's a spare set of keys," I said.

"Know where the fuse box or circuit breakers are," Kristy said.

"Ask about allergies," I said.

Mary Anne wrote furiously, using some kind of shorthand that only she can read. By the time we ran out of suggestions, she had filled up three pages with tiny print. It looked like some exotic foreign language.

"My dad has a new laser printer in his office," Mal said. "Maybe if you write that neatly, he could type it and print it out."

"Would he really do that?" Mary Anne asked.

"Hmmm . . ." Mal said. "I know. I'll offer him a free baby-sitting session or two."

"If not, I'll just print it in my best handwriting and ask my mom or dad to copy it at work," Mary Anne said.

Kristy looked deep in thought about something. "You know what, guys?" she finally said. "I hate to say it, but we'll only need a couple of people to hand out pamphlets at the booth."

That quieted everyone down. Mary Anne leafed through the record book and said, "Well, Logan, Claudia, Jessi, and Mal have jobs that day, so they can't be there." She put the book down and sighed. "It won't be much of a group activity, will it?"

"Sure it will," Kristy said. "Whoever has a job can bring their kids to the fair."

"Jessi and I are sitting for my brothers and sisters," Mal said. "We could ask them if they want to go."

"That's the kind of thing Charlotte Johanssen would *love* to do," Stacey said.

"Okay," Mary Anne replied. "If you guys do that, then that leaves Kristy and me to run the booth. Is that okay with everyone?"

We agreed to the idea, and Kristy got on the phone to Ms. Bernstein. In a few minutes, the Baby-sitters Club had officially entered its first Stoneybrook health fair.

As soon as Kristy hung up, Claudia said, "It's six o'clock! I have an idea — "

"It's *three minutes* to six," Kristy corrected her.

Claudia rolled her eyes. "Okay. In exactly *three minutes*, why don't we put in a call to Dawn in California?"

Everyone thought that was a good idea, even Kristy. And at the stroke of six, Mary Anne picked up the phone and punched in Mr. Schafer's number.

We waited silently. On the other end, the phone rang and rang and rang.

"Hello? Mr. Schafer?" Mary Anne said. We were in luck! "You just got in from the hospital? How's Jeff? . . . Dawn's there? Great! Thanks!"

There was a moment of silence, then the

loudest, happiest "Hi!" I ever heard. It was somewhere between a squeal and a word.

"How *are* you? How's Jeff? Uh-huh . . . uh-huh . . ."

"What? What?" Kristy said.

"Wait," Mary Anne held up her hand. Then, back into the phone, "Fine! We're going to have a booth in this health fair next Saturday . . . yes! . . . Here, I'll let you talk to Kristy about it."

Kristy took the phone, then Stacey, then Jessi, then Mal, then me. Mostly small talk, gossip, weather, stuff like that. It wasn't until Mary Anne got the phone back that the important question was mentioned. The question everyone seemed to be avoiding.

"So when are you coming back?" Mary Anne asked.

I couldn't hear what Dawn said, but I could tell it wasn't good. Mary Anne's face kind of sank. "Uh-huh . . . OK . . . miss you, too, Dawn. Everybody does. Give Jeff our love . . . . 'Bye!"

She hung up the phone dejectedly and said, "Jeff's recovering, but he may have to stay in the hospital longer than they first thought. Dawn wants to stay till he's home."

"She'll miss the fair!" Kristy said.

Mary Anne nodded. Her lower lip quivered a little. "Probably."

I knew that quiver. It meant a cry wasn't far behind. Sure enough, the moment I put my arm back around her, the dam broke. "It's okay," I said. "I'm sure she's learning a lot about health at the hospital."

Mary Anne started to laugh a little, and her tears soon dried up. But when the meeting ended, our good-byes were pretty somber.

I walked Mary Anne home, trying to be as cheerful as I could. But the minute I was alone, I felt a knot in the pit of my stomach. I felt bad for Mary Anne. She was taking this so seriously. But I was thinking of me, too. The longer Dawn was away, the more deeply involved in the Baby-sitters Club I became. Now I was expected to take the Hobart kids to the health fair.

What if my teammates showed up there? They probably would, too, just to show off their great pulse rates or get free food. And there I would be, surrounded by kids and the BSC. It was a little too . . . *public*.

Oh, well, it might not be so bad, I thought. Maybe they wouldn't come. Maybe Dawn would be home in time.

As long as there were maybes, I was fine. If the maybes didn't work out, well, I didn't want to think about that.

CHAPTER 7

Saturday

I sat for "our angel" (Jenny P.) and her baby sister this afternoon. It was so beautiful today that Mrs. P. insisted I take the girls outside. It sounded like a great idea, and Jenny thought so, too.

I never expected it would turn out to be such a disaster. I wouldn't be surprised if Logan never talked to me again....

I had to laugh when I read that. I had no intention of not talking to Mary Anne, even though I *had* been a little steamed about Saturday's incident.

Let me explain. First, "our angel" is what Mr. and Mrs. P. always call their daughter Jenny. Second, P. stands for Prezzioso. Third, Jenny Prezzioso is not an angel. Far from it.

What's she like? *Spoiled* is the first word that comes to mind. Before baby Andrea was born, all Jenny had to do was look at a toy and her parents would buy it for her. She had a closet full of the fanciest clothes imaginable. (It sort of makes sense if you look at Mrs. P., who dresses like she stepped out of a fashion magazine.) Jenny hated the idea of getting a baby sister. One time when Mary Anne sat for her, Jenny tore apart the baby's room from top to bottom.

But when Andrea was born, Jenny kind of lightened up. She liked the new baby and was excited about being a big sister. Now she's actually a pretty nice kid, but she's still spoiled.

When Mary Anne arrived at the Prezziosos' house on Saturday, Mrs. P. was wearing a long, flowing, silk dress. "Welcome, Mary Anne!" Mrs. P. said. "What do you think? Do I still look like a blimp?"

"What? Oh! No, not at all," Mary Anne replied. She realized Mrs. P. was talking about her pregnancy weight, which she hadn't totally lost yet. "That dress really covers it up. You look normal."

"Normal! Oh, thank goodness for that!" Mrs. P. was smiling, but I think she was expecting Mary Anne to call her ravishing or something.

Mr. P. walked in, busily trying to tie his bow tie. He was wearing a suit, with a shirt corner sticking out. "Hi, Mary Anne," he said.

"Oh, Nick, let me get that," Mrs. P. said. As she tied the bow tie, she called out, "Jenny! Mary Anne's here! Come on down!"

"Waaaaaaahhh!" came a scream from Andrea.

"Oh, darn, I woke her up," Mrs. P. said.

Jenny came running into the living room, still in her pajamas. (Mary Anne made sure to tell me they were Laura Ashley pajamas. I'm not sure what that means, but she made it seem like an important detail.) "Mommy, Andrea has a poopy diaper. Hi, Mary Anne."

"Hi. I'll take care of it," Mary Anne said.

"Thanks, dear. Afterward you can put her in the stroller and take the girls outside, okay?"

"Sure!" Mary Anne answered as she rushed to the baby's room.

She could hear Mr. P. saying to Jenny, "Now we expect our angel to behave for Mary Anne while we're at brunch."

And she could hear Jenny screaming, "I'm *not* going to listen! I *hate* daytime baby-sitters!"

A few seconds later, all she could hear was, "*Waaaaaahhhhh!*"

It didn't look like a promising day.

Mary Anne managed to change the diaper and quiet Andrea down. She carried her into the living room, where Jenny was waving to her parents through the front screen door.

Jenny turned around with a big smile on her face, as if she had had a personality transplant. "Can you lay out my clothes for me?"

"Sure," Mary Anne said. Jenny led her back upstairs and pulled open her closet. She pushed aside about a hundred almost-new outfits and pointed to a brand-new sweat suit combination. "Mommy bought me these yesterday. And new sneakers, too!"

That was why Jenny suddenly wanted to go out. Her mom must have just reminded her about the outfit (or the bribe, I should say).

Oh, well, a baby-sitter's job is to take care of the kids, not make value judgments. As for me, I think Jenny needs discipline, but that's all I'll say on the subject.

Mary Anne knew that I was working out at SMS that morning. As she was putting Andrea into the stroller, she said to Jenny, "Want to take a walk to my school? Logan's going to be practicing on the track, and we can watch him for a few minutes."

"Okay!" Jenny said. "And then can we go to the playground?"

"Sure."

"And then can we get some ice cream?"

"It'll be lunchtime by then, Jenny," Mary Anne said.

Jenny scowled. "I don't want any lunch!"

"No lunch, no ice cream," Mary Anne insisted.

"Can I have ice cream *after* lunch?"

"If you eat everything on your plate, we'll talk about it."

"Yea!" Jenny said.

And they were off. The day was clear and sunny, with a refreshing breeze, and Mary Anne felt peaceful and happy.

I felt like my legs were going to fall off. By the time Mary Anne reached the school, I had finished a two-mile warm-up run and about ten practice sprints. I was with three other guys who were going out for the team — Alex Turnbull, Bob Stillman, and Peter Hayes — and we were about to do a mile run with alternating paces. I really *felt* the fact that I hadn't exercised since the previous Tuesday.

"Yo, Logan, here comes your old lady, with

your kids," said Bob Stillman. I shot him a look, but he quickly added, "Just kidding."

Mary Anne waved to me as she rolled the stroller in front of the bleachers. She sat in the first row, being careful to turn the stroller so that the sun flap cast a shadow over the baby. Jenny sat with her for a few seconds. She waved, too, even though she doesn't know me too well.

"Hi!" I called out. Despite Bob's crack, it felt really nice to see Mary Anne there, kids or no kids.

I started to walk toward them, but then I heard Peter call out, "Hey, Bruno, you going to do this mile with us or not?"

"Oh, yeah!" I said. With a shrug and a smile, I waved back to Mary Anne, then jogged to the starting line.

"Okay," Bob said. "We'll do a two-twenty-yard jog and a two-twenty sprint, then alternate four-forties, jog and sprint, until we do four laps. Everybody got it?"

We all grunted yes. It may sound complicated if you don't run on a team, but those are standard distances, and the track is marked off so you know how far you've gone.

We were taking our starting positions when a hollow, metallic banging noise started, and we looked around. In the bleachers, Jenny had grown bored. She was running up and down, stomping her feet on the long, metal seats.

The guys looked at each other. Alex and Peter snickered. Bob murmured some snide comment, but I didn't catch it.

That's when I took over. "Okay, on your marks . . ."

"I'm king of the world!" came Jenny's voice. Out of the corner of my eyes I could see her on the top row of the bleachers. Mary Anne was desperately gesturing for her to come down.

"Get set . . ." I persisted.

"Go!" Jenny screamed.

"Go!" I said.

It wasn't the ideal way to start the run, but the guys knew enough to listen to me and not Jenny. We took off, slowly at first.

After two hundred twenty yards, or halfway around the track, we started sprinting. I was so tight, I felt as if there were claws around my legs. I gritted my teeth and pumped my aching legs as fast as they could go.

Clang! Clang! Clang! Jenny was jumping up and down on the bleachers, shouting, "Go, Logan, go! Logan's the fastest!"

Her words barely registered. My mind was blank. I was having enough trouble staring straight ahead. When the next jogging part began, I wanted to drop out and collapse. I let myself exhale loudly to force out the carbon dioxide, just like Coach Mills tells us.

"Why are you all going so slow?" Jenny was calling out.

I think that was when she started getting on my nerves.

We hit the marker for the second sprint, which was going to be a long one — one complete turn around the track. As we passed Mary Anne, I could see Jenny running back and forth, gritting her teeth (imitating us, I guess).

The minute I was past them, I felt a second wind. Maybe my legs were warming up or something, because I was able to get some extra speed. On either side of me, I could hear the sharp, frantic breathing of the other guys. We whizzed around the goalpost part of the track, everyone trying to keep pace.

On the straightaway, I began picking up more speed. To my amazement, everyone else kept pace. I dug in harder. I felt as if my lungs were going to explode. Everything in my peripheral vision was a blur.

I didn't even notice a fifth person on the track in front of us.

Jenny!

"No!" Mary Anne shrieked. "Get back here!"

"See how fast I — "

Those were the only words of Jenny's I remember hearing before I felt my legs give out. Bob had veered away from her and went plowing into me. We tumbled into the football field, taking the other two with us.

I think I blanked out for a split second, but when I got my bearings I realized I was lying flat on my stomach with Bob across my legs. The four of us were panting like crazy, too stunned and exhausted to say a word.

Jenny was staring at us, still standing, her eyes wide with fear. Somehow we had managed not to barrel into her. As Mary Anne rushed toward her, Jenny burst into tears.

Mary Anne scooped her up. "Jenny, what on earth — "she began.

"I — I wanted to *run!*" Jenny wailed through her tears.

Around me, the other guys were climbing to their feet. "This is no place for kids!" Alex Turnbull said.

"I'm sorry," Mary Anne replied, backing away. She looked as frightened as Jenny did. "I guess this wasn't such a good idea."

"Good guess," Bob muttered.

"I'll take the girls home now," Mary Anne said. "Sorry."

I felt torn. I wanted to run after her and tell her it was okay. After all, it wasn't really her fault. Who would have thought Jenny would do something stupid like that? On the other hand, I was pretty annoyed at Jenny. We were lucky there hadn't been a serious accident.

"Sorry about that, guys," was the only thing I could think of saying.

"Just can't keep the girls away, huh?" Bob said with a sly grin.

"Of all ages," Alex added.

Peter looked with mock horror at an elderly woman who was walking by the school. "Quick, hide him. Look who's coming!"

"Not funny, guys," I said with a sigh. "Come on, let's get in a couple more sprints."

CHAPTER 8

"She is not!"

"She is!"

"Is not!"

"Is!"

The Hobart boys were having a conference. The topic was whether or not their older brother Ben was Mallory Pike's friend or *boy*friend.

It was Monday, and I was sitting for three Hobarts: Mathew, Johnny, and James. Ben was riding bikes with Mallory somewhere. And that was the center of the controversy.

In case you're wondering, Ben and Mallory *are* only friends. But don't try to tell James that. With Ben away, he was playing the sage older brother.

"You guys just don't *know* about boyfriend-girlfriend stuff," he said.

"We do so!" Mathew protested.

"Yeah!" Johnny echoed.

"Oh, yeah?" James shot back. "Okay, how

old do you start having girlfriends?"

Mathew and Johnny looked at him blankly. "Um . . . twenty-five?" Mathew guessed.

James rolled his eyes. "No, you numskull. Eleven! Before you're eleven, girls are friends. After eleven, they're *girlfriends*. Everybody knows that."

Johnny and Mathew nodded. They looked as if they'd just received the wisdom of the ages.

I was steering clear of this conversation. My legs felt tight, so I was doing stretches on the kitchen floor.

"Logan?" I heard Mathew say.

I turned around in midstretch. "Yeah?"

"James says . . ." Mathew's voice trailed off. "What are you doing?"

"Stretching," I answered. "I have to get my legs in shape for track tryouts."

"What's track?" Johnny asked.

James blurted out excitedly, "You're trying out for the track team?"

"First question first," I said, turning to Johnny. "Track is a name for a bunch of different sports, like running, jumping, pole vaulting, and relay racing." Then I said to James. "And the answer is yes, I am trying out. I've been practicing at the SMS track."

"The one that goes all the way around the football field?" Mathew said.

"Yup."

"Wow! *I* want to run around that!" Johnny said. "I'll go sooo fast."

"I'll go faster!" Mathew said.

James was practically jumping with excitement. "Can you take us there?"

"Yeah!" Mathew piped up.

"Yeah!" Johnny echoed.

Now they were all jumping around. I didn't exactly have much choice. If I said no, I'd be the meanest person this side of Ebenezer Scrooge.

Besides, there was no football practice on Monday, and I was pretty sure the track would be empty. If I was lucky, I could make the kids happy *and* avoid being seen.

"All right, all right," I said, standing up.

"Yeaaaa!" the brothers yelled.

"We'll start with a cross-country run, from here to SMS!" I said. "It's just a few blocks, and I don't want any show-offs. We'll all run at the same speed."

"But Johnny's too slow!" James whined.

"Am not!" Johnny retorted.

"James, it's not that he's slower, really," I said. "It's that your legs are longer than his. It's all relative."

"Yeah!" Johnny trumpeted. "We're all relatives!"

The kids were wearing sneakers, so I

71

grabbed the house keys and said, "Let's go!"

With screams and squeals, they ran out the back door. I quickly wrote a note to the Hobarts, in case they came home early. Then I locked up and began jogging toward the school with the kids. Actually it was more like walking, because I made sure to keep Johnny's pace. Mathew and James were pretty good about staying with us, although I had to call them back a couple of times.

When we reached the school, I breathed a sigh of relief. The track *was* empty. "Charge!" I called out.

This time Mathew and James sprinted ahead. They began running around the track as fast as they could — and they ran out of breath about a quarter of the way around.

Johnny joined them a few seconds later. He began doing a silly, zigzaggy run, with his arms and legs flailing all over the place.

Mathew and James followed behind, imitating him, and James plowed into a low hurdle, knocking it over. "Watch it, you guys!" I said.

"What are these things?" James asked.

"Hurdles,"I replied. "You're supposed to jump over them. Watch."

Now, the low hurdles is never going to be my main event, but I know how to run them. So I picked up the one James had knocked over, then backed up to prepare.

There were six of them in a row, spaced far enough apart for about four running paces. I eyed them carefully to psych myself up, then said, "Okay, here's how you begin a race. First the referee says, 'On your mark!' and you go like this." I crouched into a racing stance, one foot behind the other, hands on the ground, elbows slightly bent.

"Then he says, 'Get set!' " I leaned forward, lifting my rear end and straightening my elbows.

"Then 'Go!' " To a chorus of loud cheers, I sprinted toward the hurdles. I could feel my hamstrings aching. The first hurdle felt awful, but I cleared it. In fact, I cleared all but the second to last.

When I finished, I turned and raised my fists in triumph. The Hobart boys were jumping up and down like crazy. But when I jogged toward them, I realized they weren't cheering for me.

"I want to go first!" Mathew said.

"Age before beauty!" Johnny said.

"You don't even know what that means!" James said.

"Whoa!" I cut in. "I hate to say it, but none of you is really big enough to clear these. Go ahead, James, try."

I have to hand it to him. He gave the first

one a good shot, but landed splat on the ground, laughing.

I had a better idea. "Let's have a relay race!" I said, picking up a foot-long stick from the ground. "Here's our baton. See this blue line?" I pointed to a marker on the track. "I'll start here. You guys find the next three markers, and each of you stand on one. I'll run to whoever's on the next marker, and then he runs to the next one, and so on."

They eagerly followed my instructions — almost. I passed to James, who promptly dropped the baton. He recovered it and ran to Mathew, who started running too soon. By the time Mathew got the baton, he and James were right behind Johnny, who grabbed it out of their hands — and ran off the track and across the football field, giggling.

"Get him!" I yelled, and we all chased after Johnny, finally tumbling on the grass in a fit of laughter.

Next they wanted to practice the positions for "on your marks, get set, go!" We lined up on the track and I called out the commands. They did the crouch, the lift, and the takeoff. That was *all* they were supposed to do, but of course they insisted on having a race each time.

And each time they came back to their marks, they were more and more breathless.

Finally, after about the tenth time, Johnny said, "I'm tired!"

"Yeah?" I replied. "Maybe we better head back."

"No, one more time!" James insisted.

"Yeah, we can do it without Johnny!" Mathew said.

"No!" Johnny protested. "I'll do it, too!"

We lined up again. The boys were red-faced with exhaustion. "On your marks!" I said.

They crouched. I could see Mathew's left arm buckle a little.

"Get set!"

They lifted. This time Johnny's right leg buckled.

"Go!"

James lurched ahead. I could see he had "world record" on his mind. But his knees weren't ready. He stumbled to the left, and ran into Mathew.

Mathew lost his balance. He reached out, grabbing Johnny and pulling him to the ground. I was on the far left, and the weight of three Hobarts was too much for me.

We landed in a heap on the track.

"Pile up!" James screamed.

Giggling, Mathew and Johnny decided they would attack me together. "Tickle monster!" Mathew shouted.

They came at my rib cage with their fingers.

I don't usually think of myself as ticklish, but they were doing a great job. I tried to wriggle away, laughing uncontrollably. "Stop stop stop stop stop stop!" I said.

"Hey, what is this, a day care center?"

The new voice was like a slap in the face. Mathew and Johnny whirled around to look. I scrambled to my feet.

There, standing with their hands on their hips, were Alex Turnbull, Peter Hayes, and three other guys in running clothes.

"Oh, sorry," I replied. "I was just showing them the track."

"Uh, would you mind baby-sitting someplace else so we can *run*?" Bob said. "Someplace far away so no little kid wanders into our path?"

"We were about to go home anyway," I said.

"Good," Bob replied.

"Hey, Logan, you going to bring some kids to the tryouts, too?" Alex called out.

"It's not Logan, it's *Lois*!" Peter added. "Lois, the new Baby-sitters Club member!"

The guys laughed as if this were the funniest joke ever made. I tell you, I was boiling mad inside. I wanted to slug all of them, but I couldn't. Like it or not, the Hobart boys were my main concern.

So I swallowed my anger. Buried it deep

down, somewhere near my ankles. "Come on, kids," I said.

We left silently. Behind us, my former friends were still joking, but I was tuning them out.

The Hobarts were silent almost all the way home. Like me, they just stared at the sidewalk as we walked.

"Logan," James finally said, as we approached their house, "why were those guys teasing you like that?"

"They called you Lois," Johnny added.

I took a deep breath. "Some guys — not all, just some — think that guys shouldn't babysit. They think it's something girls do, and it's not as important as, you know, *boy* stuff, like sports."

"You think it's important, don't you?" Mathew asked.

"Sure I do. But I'm different from those guys, I guess, and that makes them try to act superior. So they tease me."

James nodded. "Yeah, my brothers and I used to get teased all the time, right?"

"Yes," Mathew and Johnny agreed.

"People used to make fun of our accent," James continued. "They thought we were freaks or something. They were being stupid."

"But we stood up to them," Mathew said, "and they started being nicer."

"It's bad to tease," Johnny said.

"It is," I agreed. "I think people do it when they feel scared, or when they think something's being taken away from them. You guys know Jessi Ramsey?"

"The baby-sitter?" James asked.

"Yeah. People were mean to her just because she's black. And people make fun of my brother Hunter all the time because he has allergies that make him talk funny."

"It's dumb," Mathew said. "I used to tease a kid back in Australia, but I don't tease anybody anymore."

The Hobarts' car was in the driveway, and as we walked up the lawn, Mr. Hobart came to the screen door. "Hi, mates!" he called out. "Have a good day?"

His sons rushed inside to tell him their news. I followed them in, politely collected my pay, and said good-bye.

" 'Bye!" the boys echoed. Mathew added, "Good luck with the track tryouts!"

"Thanks," I replied, "but I'll see you before then. Remember, I'm taking you guys to the health fair on Saturday."

"Hey, awesome!" Mathew said with a grin.

I waved and headed out the door.

I wasn't sure *awesome* was the right word. If I had one more scene like today's, *gruesome* would be more like it.

CHAPTER 9

It felt great to put on my cleats and my padding. Tuesday afternoon was my first football practice in a week, and I had missed being there.

At least I thought I had. My feeling changed the minute King walked into the locker room. "Hey, look who's here! Lois Bruno, the baby-sitter!"

"Eeeek! There's a girl in the locker room!" Pete Black screeched, pulling his towel tightly around him.

"Very funny, guys," I said, trying to be a sport about it. In the back of my mind, I was furious at Bob, or Alex, or whichever of those guys had told King about my new nickname. What was I now, the talk of the school?

Just because I do a little baby-sitting?

"Don't listen to those jerks," Austin Bentley said as he sat at his locker, three down from mine.

"I'm not," I answered. "I don't care what they say."

Okay, I lied. But I figured by saying that, I might actually start to feel it was true.

I walked out to the field with Austin. A bunch of the guys were already tossing the ball around, running sprints through tires, bashing into padded dummies, the usual fun-filled stuff.

Austin picked a football off the ground. "Go out for a pass!" he said.

I sprinted downfield and turned. Austin's throw sailed over my head and hit the ground a few yards in front of me. It bounced away, toward a cluster of my teammates on the sidelines.

Harry Nolan, one of our wide receivers, grabbed it and said, "Nice of you to show up."

He tossed the ball to a tackle named Steve Randazzo, who said, "Hey, Harry, let's give it back to her." Then, turning to me, he tossed the ball with an awkward, slow underhand motion, as if he were throwing to a baby. "Here, Lois, catch."

This was going way too far, and I didn't have to take it. But before I could say a thing, Coach Mills blew his whistle. "Okay, line up for calisthenics!" he called out.

As we trudged into formation, I ended up next to King. "Ew, who wants to play football with a *girl*?" he muttered, changing places with Austin.

"Shut your mouth, you orangutan," Austin said.

That was good for a few laughs, which made King scowl and say, "What's the matter, Lois can't talk for herself?"

I was beginning to lose it. These guys had singled me out, and they weren't going to let up. I'd seen them do it to others, and I knew they only got worse if you showed any emotion. "King," I said, as cool as I could be, "cram it."

"Ooooh," came a few voices behind us.

"Push-up position!" Coach Mills yelled. "One . . . two . . . three . . ."

I don't love doing push-ups, but I was happy for the silence. After push-ups, we went through sit-ups and jumping jacks. It was during the sit-ups, I think, that I first noticed Mary Anne in the stands.

Seeing her really lifted my mood, but I have to admit, the first thing I did was look around for kids. Fortunately, she was alone.

I hoped she hadn't been there when the insults were flying, but as it turned out, it didn't matter. There were plenty more to come.

In the first play of our intrasquad game, I went after a pass and fell. Harry Nolan was covering me, and as he ran by he said, "What's the matter, the kids wearing you out?"

Later on, King tackled me on a hand-off, and while we were on the ground he said, "So, what's this I hear about you joining the Girl Scouts, too?"

In the second half, just as I was about to catch a long, perfect pass that would have been a sure touchdown, I heard Pete Black yell, "Watch that nail polish!"

I dropped the ball.

As I headed back to the line of scrimmage, Coach Mills walked up to me. "What's going on here?" he asked.

"What do you mean?"

"I mean, you seem a little out of shape — and you look mad at the world. You feeling all right?"

"Just a little rusty, that's all," I said. "And, you know, mad at *myself* for not being in shape."

"Hey, don't sweat it, Logan," the coach said, patting me on the back. "Just let me see you at practice regularly, okay? And if you can make it Saturday morning I'm going to have some full-uniform wind sprints — strictly optional."

"Right, Coach," I replied. I didn't say a thing about the health fair. Another practice down the drain.

After Coach Mills walked away, I could hear Steve crack, "What's up, Lois, secret baby-sitting talk with the coach? You going to take care of his kids tonight?"

That did it. I whirled around. A few other guys were standing next to him, grinning at his joke. "Look, you idiots, mind your own business! Just cut it, okay? It's not funny any more!"

"Who-o-o-oa, just kidding," Steve said. "Where's your sense of humor?"

"Yeah, Lo — Logan," Harry said (I could tell he had almost said *Lois*).

I turned and walked away. My sense of humor was gone, thanks to their "jokes." I played out the rest of the game, then stormed into the locker by myself and changed without taking a shower. I didn't even want to talk to Austin.

Mary Anne was waiting by the locker room door when I came out. She had this kind, sympathetic look on her face, which should have made me feel better but somehow made things worse.

I tried to smile but probably didn't even manage that. Mary Anne walked out of school with me. She put her arm around my shoulder when we got outside, but she didn't say a word as we walked home, and neither did I.

On my front porch, I finally turned to her

and said, "Sorry I'm so grumpy. Those guys really got on my nerves."

Mary Anne nodded. "I know. Mine, too. Some friends."

She stood there, smiling warmly. I could tell she wanted to be invited inside.

Don't get me wrong, I *wanted* to invite her, but I couldn't. The way I was feeling, I just needed to eat, plod through my homework, and fall asleep. I didn't need sympathy or pity or cheering up. I didn't need to think about anything serious at all.

I gave Mary Anne a quick kiss and said, "Thanks for coming to practice. I'll call you tonight, okay?"

I could see disappointment flicker across her face, but only for a split second. She squeezed my hand and said, "Okay. And don't worry about . . . you know."

"Yeah," I said. " 'Bye."

" 'Bye."

I walked inside and heard my mom call from the kitchen, "Is that you, Logan?"

"Yeah," I said.

"How was practice?"

"Fine."

"Can you help me fix a salad?"

"As soon as I put my books in my room."

There was a sudden burst of footsteps from

the stairs. "Logan! Logan!" Kerry and Hunter screamed.

"Hey," I greeted them.

"I'm having a birthday party for Tricera!" Hunter said, holding up a plastic dinosaur with a Dixie cup on its head. (His dinosaur's last name is Tops, for obvious reasons.)

"Great," I said.

"Do you have to baby-sit tonight?" Kerry asked.

I half expected her to call me Lois. "No," I answered, not even looking at her.

"Goody!" she replied.

I walked into my room, plopped my books on the desk, and plopped myself in my chair. I was exhausted, plus I could feel a headache coming on, not to mention all the muscle aches in my arms and legs. I exhaled loudly, leaned forward, and covered my face with my hands. I was kind of hoping Kerry and Hunter would be gone by the time I looked up.

No such luck. They were both staring at me curiously. "Are you okay, Logan?" Kerry asked.

I just shrugged. A lot of help it would be to tell a nine-year-old and a five-year-old my problems. "I have to help Mom," I said.

"I'll help, too," Kerry added.

"Me, too," Hunter echoed.

They followed me downstairs. Mom and Dad managed to find jobs for them to do, and we sat down to a dinner of leftover meatloaf and gravy.

About halfway through, Dad said, "You're awfully quiet tonight, Logan."

"Yeah," I said. "The guys at practice were giving me grief about baby-sitting."

Dad chuckled. "Well, boys will be boys. Just wait till one of them has a girlfriend."

That wasn't exactly the point, but I didn't have the energy to say anything about it. Instead I ate the rest of my dinner, nodding at whatever anyone else had to say.

My grouchiness stayed with me all night. I could tell Mom and Dad were concerned, but they left me alone. As for Kerry and Hunter . . . well, in the middle of math homework (bo-ring!), I heard a knock on my door and Kerry peeked in. "Hi!" she said. "I thought you might be hungry."

She brought me a little bowl of yogurt with granola mixed in and put it on my desk.

"Thanks," I said.

Then I heard a growly voice saying, "I'm going to get Logan!"

Hunter came into the room on his hands and knees, with a plastic tyrannosaurus and good old Tricera Tops. He thrust the tyrannosaurus forward and let out a roar.

"No! No!" he said in his Tricera voice. "I'll protect him." He made Tricera attack the tyrannosaurus with its horns.

"Ow! Ow!" he yelped, as the tyrannosaurus.

I had to laugh. I could tell Hunter and Kerry knew something was wrong, and they wanted to cheer me up. "Thanks, guys," I said, "for the food *and* the protection."

I felt a little better after that, but when I went to bed that night, I couldn't fall asleep for a long time. This split schedule wasn't working out. Something had to give. I might have to make a choice between sitting and sports.

I had a feeling I knew what was going to win. And it wasn't going to make Mary Anne very happy.

CHAPTER 10

Monday

*I know we're sup-
posed to write about
our experiences at
the health fair. But
Mal and I aren't.*

We're going to write about what happened
beforehand. Like a prologue.

*We sat for Mal's brothers
and sisters. And getting
them out of the house
to go to the fair was
sort of like...*

Torture.

*I wasn't going to say it.
I'm glad you did.*

Well, after Saturday, I think Jessi and I
agree on how to get a group of kids to go
someplace they may not like.

Yeah. Force them.

There was one major problem with the health fair idea, and no one in the BSC had thought of it.

To kids, it sounded boring.

Jessi and Mallory discovered that the hard way on the day of the fair. As I mentioned before, Mal has seven brothers and sisters. Three of them are triplets: Adam, Jordan, and Byron (they're ten years old). Next are Vanessa (nine), Nicky (eight), Margo (seven), and Claire (five).

Getting seven kids to do *anything* is a major triumph. Getting them to do something they don't want to do . . . Well, let's just say I was glad I was sitting for the Hobarts that day.

Jessi arrived at the Pikes' while the kids were eating breakfast. They were all huddled over their food, having a discussion.

"Is maple syrup a health food?" Margo asked.

"It's natural, that much I know," Mallory replied. "But I'm not sure you'd call it a health food."

"Bacon is," Nicky said.

"How do you know?" Adam asked.

" 'Cause James Hobart says his mom says it makes him grow big and strong," Nicky retorted.

"That doesn't mean — " Mal began.

"How about ice cream?" Vanessa asked.

"Of course not!" Mal said.

"Well, it has milk in it," Vanessa replied.

"Can I have some ice cream at the fair?" Claire asked.

"There's no ice cream at a health fair, dum-dum," Jordan said.

"I'm not a dum-dum!" Claire cried.

"I guess that means no cotton candy, either," Adam said.

"No way," Jordan said. "There's probably just rice cakes and low-fat frozen yogurt. Alfalfa flavor."

"Ew!" Margo said.

"Well, *I'm* going to go on the rides!" Claire asked. "You'll take me, right, Jessi?"

Jessi shrugged helplessly. "No rides, Claire."

"No rides, no good food, no nothing," Adam said. "Why do we have to go to this dumb fair?"

"It'll be a good experience for you," Mal told him. "You'll learn a lot."

"School is for learning," Jordan said. "Fairs are supposed to be fun."

"Maybe it will be fun," Jessi suggested.

"Yeah, right," Adam muttered. "It's just going to be a bunch of nurses and doctors giving you checkups."

"We're going to the doctor?" Claire said, her voice filled with panic.

"No!" Mal exclaimed. "Now will you guys finish your breakfasts and get ready to leave?"

What a zoo. Reluctantly, the Pikes dug into their food again, but slooowly. Vanessa began cutting her waffle into smaller and smaller pieces, Claire mashed her scrambled eggs with her fork, Jordan peeled the crust off his toast, Adam slurped the milk from his cereal bowl and insisted on more.

Mal said getting them away from the table was like moving a mountain. Jessi thought it was more like moving seven mountains. Whatever, the kids finally began to get ready.

Sort of.

"Can't we watch the *Peter Pan* video?" Nicky asked as he brought his bowl to the sink.

"Why can't we go to the playground?" Margo asked.

"Or find a *real* fair," Claire said.

"Bathroom time!" Mal announced, ignoring the requests.

"I get the downstairs bathroom first!" Nicky called.

"Share it," Mal said.

"No!" Nicky insisted urgently. "I need . . . privacy." He looked at Jessi and blushed.

"Okay, some of you can go upstairs," Mal said.

"Not me!" chorused six voices.

"Let's choose straws," Adam suggested. He pulled some toothpicks out of a kitchen drawer and counted out six. Then he broke one, mixed them up, and held them out so they looked the same size.

Mal and Jessi just sighed with resignation. They watched as Vanessa "won" and trudged upstairs.

Margo ran to her room, yelling, "Want to hear me read *Sneetches*? I can read the whole thing!"

"Just for a minute — " Mal began to say.

She was cut off by a crash from the play room near the kitchen. Jessi ran there to see Claire in the middle of a pile of spilled Lego blocks. "I'm going to build a city!" she said gleefully.

Well, Claire never got to build that city, and Margo read only as far as Sylvester McMonkey McBean's entrance. Jessi and Mal, champion baby-sitters, somehow lured them all out of the house.

But the torment wasn't over yet.

As they walked across the Pikes' front lawn, Vanessa knelt down and exclaimed, "Ooh, look, a firefly in the daytime!"

Claire and Byron began running toward her, but Mal pulled them back. "Come on, everybody, let's sing a marching song."

"Yuck, I hate that," Nicky replied.

"How about the 'Following the Leader' song from *Peter Pan*?" Adam suggested.

"Great idea," Jessi said. "I'll lead."

"No, me!" Adam insisted.

Adam and Margo started singing, " 'We're following the leader, the leader, the leader . . .' "

Behind them, Nicky crouched like some kind of monster and sang, "We're swallowing the leader, the leader, the leader; we're swallowing the leader and throwing him up!"

"Ew, that's disgusting!" Byron said.

"You're doing that because you don't know the real words," Adam said.

"Do too!" Nicky snapped.

"Sing it the right way, guys," Mal said.

The triplets, Nicky, and Margo half-heartedly sang with Jessi and Mal. Vanessa lagged behind them, looking up into the trees and talking to herself.

Actually, she was composing nature poems. Jessi heard her reciting: "Firefly, firefly in the day. Will you stay or go away?" Stuff like that.

An older man passed them on the sidewalk and smiled. "Fine singing group you got there," he said.

"You're a silly-billy-goo-goo," Claire told him. (That's one of her favorite expressions.)

Mal was at the end of her rope. "Claire,

that's not nice!" she said. She would have said something *much* stronger if they hadn't turned onto Atlantic Avenue just then and seen the shopping center. Over the main entrance was a sign that said WELCOME TO THE FIFTH ANNUAL STONEYBROOK HEALTH FAIR.

As soon as they walked through, Margo shouted, "Look! There's Mary Anne and Kristy!"

For the first time all morning, the kids actually began running.

As Jessi and Mal watched the Pike kids near the BSC booth, they looked at each other and laughed. "If they *do* end up having a good time here," Jessi said, "I'll eat alfalfa ice cream."

Monday

Okay, my turn. I can't let Mal and Jessi hog the whole book. Just kidding. Anyway, I have to say our booth was a big success. We gave out practically all our fliers. Get ready to be unbelievably busy, you guys! As for what happened with Logan, well, I guess some things are just out of our control...

I'll explain that last remark later. In the meantime, I'll just say that Saturday was not my favorite day of all time — although it was a great day for the BSC.

By the time the Pikes arrived, the fair had been going for a half hour. Kristy and Mary Anne had already given out a dozen or so pamphlets, and they were deep in conversation with a couple who'd just moved into town.

"This is a great idea, honey," the man was saying to his wife as he looked through a pamphlet. "We can keep this out for sitters when they come."

"As a matter of fact," Kristy said, *"we're* sitters. Here's our number."

She handed them a flier just as the Pike kids ran to the booth, screaming hellos. "Hi, you guys!" Mary Anne said.

"We sit for a lot of kids in the neighborhood," Kristy explained to the couple. "As you can see."

"And you do it very well, it seems," the woman said with a smile. "We'll be in touch."

As they walked away, Kristy said, "Perfect timing! You guys are the greatest advertising!"

"Maybe we should go back and do it again when the next family comes," Jessi said, as she and Mal approached the booth.

"*You* can direct them, Jessi," Mal said. "I'll watch."

"Guess what, Mal?" Kristy said. "Everyone loves the way the pamphlets look." (Mal's dad had been able to get someone at his office to type them up on the laser printer and staple them together.)

"Great!" Mal replied.

"What do you think of our booth?" Mary Anne asked.

The booth, by the way, was basically a card table and two chairs. The BSC fliers were stacked on the left side of the table, the pamphlets on the right, and a big sign was draped over the front.

The sign was Claudia's work, and it looked like this:

"It's fantastic," Jessi said. "We noticed it the minute we came in."

Margo's voice interrupted the conversation: "Mallory, can I have my blood pressure taken at the bloodmobile?"

"Me too!" most of the other Pike kids piped up.

"If you want," Mal said. "Just line up together and don't fight."

The bloodmobile was next to the BSC booth, and a woman and man in hospital whites began taking the Pike kids' blood pressure and pulse. Next to them was a team of people demonstrating CPR with different-sized plastic dummies. Then there was a nutrition booth with information about the *real* four food groups; a group of cooks preparing food in a wok under a sign that said MACROBIOTIC CUISINE; a wilderness-survival group signing up high-school-age kids for hikes; and booths set up by the local YMCA, a running-gear company from Stamford, a chiropractor, and a pediatrician, among others.

In a nearby corner of the shopping center, the "Tommy Anatomy" show was about to begin. "Tommy Anatomy" is a local actor who puts on a musical about the human body, mostly at elementary schools and playgrounds. He wears a costume with the human body painted on it —bones, organs, tissues, blood vessels, the works —and uses it to point out things as he sings to a tape recording.

"Ladies and gentlemen and bodies of all ages!" he announced. "I'm Tommy Anatomy, but my friends call me Gross! Let me sing you a song that'll touch your hearts, stimulate your minds, warm your bones, and get your blood flowing!"

Corny, I know, but immediately kids gathered around. He was a popular event, but even during his show, a bunch of people visited the BSC booth. Among them were Claudia (with Jamie Newton), the Ohdners, the Papadakises, and the Braddocks. A lot of people Kristy didn't even know came, too. ("New business, a good sign," she insisted). At one point, a young couple wandered over and began looking at the pamphlet. Kristy figured they were college-age.

"Are you guys baby-sitters?" she asked.

"Uh, no." The woman smiled. "I'm two months pregnant."

"Sorry!" Kristy said, laughing. "In that case, take one of these, too." She handed the woman a flier.

After they left, Mary Anne said, "I don't know how you do that, Kristy. Just blurt things out like that. And people don't even get mad at you."

Kristy shrugged. "What's to get mad at? I'm lovable, funny, smart — "

"And conceited," came Stacey's voice.

Kristy turned to see Stacey and Charlotte Johanssen standing behind her. "Hi, Stace!" Kristy said. Then she looked at Charlotte and said, "You think I'm lovable, right, Char?"

"Oh, brother," Charlotte murmured.

Everyone laughed, especially Kristy. (It's true that she has a big ego, but she does have a sense of humor about it.)

That was about when Kristy saw me. Johnny Hobart was riding on my back, pretending to be a cowboy, while Mathew galloped along next to us. "Thataway, Logan-horse!" Johnny called out, pointing to the booth.

"Giddyup, Logan!" Kristy shouted.

"Me too!" Mathew shouted back. "I'm a horse, too!"

"Careful, Math — !" Kristy saw that Mathew was about to gallop into someone, but by the time she warned him, it was too late.

"Oops!" Mathew said, bouncing off a person about a foot taller than him. "Sorry."

Clarence King turned around. He didn't look at Mathew. I don't know if he even felt the collision.

Instead, he grinned at me and said, "Hey-y-y-y, how's the little mommy today? Guess you don't need wind sprints, playing horsie like that."

Pete Black, Harry Nolan, and Irv Hirsch were with him, snickering at King's incomparable wit. They were still in football gear, even though sprints had ended. I guess they figured they looked cool.

100

"Uh-oh," Kristy said to Mary Anne. "I smell trouble."

You know what? I'm glad Johnny was on my back. If he hadn't been, I think I would have decked King right then and there, or at least tried to. I was that angry.

"Who writes your material, King?" I asked, somehow unclenching my teeth. "It's stale. Try again."

I think I confused him. His eyes kind of went blank, then he said to Pete, "Hey, let's show Lois the booth on health careers for women."

"Those morons," Mary Anne said. She started to come around the table, but Kristy held her back.

"Don't, Mary Anne," she said. "If they see you trying to help him, they'll just get worse. Logan can handle it."

That was good advice. I was glad Mary Anne was concerned, but King was just waiting for any excuse to be obnoxious.

So I thought I'd beat him to it. "You know, *Clarence*," I said, "if you doubled your brainpower, you'd be a halfwit."

"Whew," Irv said, pretending to be shocked, "are you going to take that, King?"

King smiled tensely. "I don't hit *girls*," he replied.

Before I could respond to that, Johnny

crouched down and whispered in my ear, "Um, Logan? I have to go to the bathroom."

Pete found that uproariously funny. He turned away, trying (barely) to hide his laughter.

"You heard the kid," King said with a smirk. "Go take him to the potty."

I could feel Johnny squirming on my back. Mathew was holding my hand, looking scared and helpless. And I did the only thing I could do.

I walked toward the men's room with the Hobarts. I tried as hard as I could to tune out the gale of laughter behind me.

And you know what the worst thing was? I just hated, *hated* the fact that that pigskinhead King was getting the last laugh.

CHAPTER 12

"I *don't* go to the potty. Only *little* boys go to the potty!"

Guess what? I wasn't the only one upset. King had insulted Johnny Hobart's big-boyhood — and Johnny wasn't going to take it sitting down.

At least, not sitting down on a potty.

"He didn't really mean it," I said, trying to sound like I was telling the truth. "He knows you're a big boy."

"I am!" Johnny agreed. "I can use the toilet like a man, too! Go get him, Logan. I'll show him!"

"Not now," I said. "Let's just go inside and get it over with, okay?"

The men's room was a small cinderblock building on one end of the shopping center. As we neared the entrance, Johnny started wriggling like crazy. "No . . . no!"

"No *what*?" I asked.

"Let me down!"

I did, and Johnny stood next to Mathew, between me and the entrance. "We're allowed to go inside by *ourselves*," Johnny said defiantly. "Right, Mathew?"

"Uh-huh," Mathew agreed.

The two of them stood there like miniature soldiers guarding a fort. As upset as I was, I didn't have the heart to say no. I knew Johnny's pride was hurt, and he needed *something* to make him feel strong.

Boy, did I understand how that felt.

"All right," I said. "You can both go in. But Mathew is officially in charge. Mathew, you keep an eye on things, okay?"

"Yes," Mathew replied.

"Okay," Johnny said solemnly, as if we'd just negotiated an international treaty. "Now you wait over there."

He pointed to a bench in front of a nearby shop. I walked over to it as the boys marched proudly into the men's room. They disappeared behind an outdoor metal partition and through an entrance.

I sat staring at that partition, not wanting to move my gaze for a second.

To tell you the truth, I didn't feel real comfortable about this arrangement. I kept wondering what Mr. and Mrs Hobart would think if they found out. What I was doing was *not* responsible baby-sitting.

But I didn't want to doubt my instincts. Johnny needed this, I said to myself. Besides, what could possibly happen?

However, after about five minutes, I started to feel nervous. But I calmed myself down and sat tight. The last thing I wanted to do was march in there and completely blow Johnny's trust in me. He was just taking awhile. It happens to all of us.

I checked my watch once, twice, three times.

After ten minutes, I began imagining Johnny's picture on the side of a milk carton.

I'd waited long enough. I stood up and walked behind the partition and into the building. I was in a short entryway. Beyond it, a carpeted hallway led to the left.

Bang!

"Give it back!"

It was Mathew's voice. My heart started to race. I sprang around the corner, clenching my fists.

The hallway stretched in front of me. Three snack machines lined the right side. A doorway was to the left.

And there was Mathew, standing in front of a candy machine with his fist in the air.

"Oh!" he gasped, jumping back. "You scared me, Logan!"

I let out a deep sigh of relief. "Sorry," I said. "Where's Johnny?"

Mathew pointed to the door down the hall. "Still inside," he muttered. Then he started yanking one of the knobs on the machine. "This dumb machine took my money. I put in the right amount, and I pulled the knob for a Milky Way, and nothing came out! No candy bar, no money!"

"Maybe it ran out, Mathew," I suggested. "Do you want to try another kind, or do you want your change back?"

"Another kind," Mathew said with a frown. "Three Musketeers."

I pulled out the Three Musketeers knob and a candy bar clunked down into the chute. Mathew's face lit up.

"There," I said. "Now will you please go inside and get your brother? He must have fallen asleep in there."

"Okay." Mathew scampered through the door, unwrapping his candy and calling out, "Johnny!"

I heard the metallic slam of a stall door.

"Johnny!"

Another slam, then another.

"Johnny?"

The last one was a question more than a

shout. I didn't like the sound of it.

Mathew came running out. "I can't find Johnny!" he cried.

I rushed past him into the room. "Come on, Johnny!" I said. "This isn't funny."

My voice echoed against the tiled walls. I pulled open one stall after the other. I looked under the sinks. I even opened up the wastebasket and pushed aside the pile of paper towels.

No Johnny.

I felt my stomach do a flip-flop. "Come with me!" I said, grabbing Mathew's hand. We ran out the door, then took a right down the hallway, went back through the entrance and into the shopping center.

"Johnny?" we called, looking left and right. We scanned Tommy Anatomy's audience. We checked the food concession.

When we arrived at the BSC booth, Mary Anne was looking worried. She'd been watching us while Kristy was talking to a group of SMS kids.

"Logan, what's going on? Where's Johnny?" she asked.

"I can't find him," I said, shocked at the words as they came out of my mouth. "I — I watched him go into the men's room, and I didn't take my eyes off the entrance once, and — "

"You let him go in by himself?"

That was Kristy. She had turned around to listen. The people she'd been talking to were now staring at me. I felt like a chainsaw murderer or something.

"No!" I cried. "He went in with — what's the difference, Kristy? I have to find him!"

I turned to leave. Kristy shouted after me, "There's a lost-children area near the cineplex!"

I veered in that direction, with Mathew close behind me. When I reached it, the man in charge just shook his head. Then he asked for Johnny's name.

I gave it to him, told him I was with the BSC, and ran back across the shopping center, shouting, "Johnny! Johnny!"

"Will Johnny Hobart please go to the Baby-sitters Club booth," came the lost-children man's voice over a loudspeaker.

People started looking around. I could hear a buzz of concern. Even Tommy Anatomy stopped his show momentarily.

Mathew and I peered into every group of people, every corner. When we reached the other end of the shopping center, we ducked into a toy store and searched it thoroughly. Then we tried the pet shop, the soda fountain at Woolworth's, the comic book shop, even the barber.

No luck anywhere.

I was freaking out. Kristy was right. What kind of baby-sitter would do what I had done? Where did I get off thinking I could be responsible for kids? What was I going to tell Mr. and Mrs. Hobart?

I tried to throw those thoughts out of my mind. I had to keep looking, and the pizza shop was one of the only logical places left. Keeping Mathew by my side, I ran toward it, hoping against hope that Johnny was talking his way into a slice and a soda.

When I spotted a pay phone right, I stopped short. "Wait!" I ordered Mathew, determined not to let *him* get away. I fished around in my pocket for some change.

"What are you going to do?" Mathew asked, his eyes wide with panic.

"I'm calling the police!" I said.

But the minute I picked up the receiver, I heard Mary Anne's voice.

"Logan, stop!" she was shouting. "Come here!"

Mathew and I turned around. We couldn't see the entire BSC booth, but we could see Mary Anne poking her head around some people and waving frantically to us.

I dropped the phone and grabbed Mathew by the hand. Somehow I managed not to yank his arm off as I sprinted toward Mary Anne.

CHAPTER 13

My jaw dropped when we arrived at the booth. There was Johnny, making a paper airplane out of a BSC flier. There were Kristy and Mary Anne, looking relieved.

And there was King, leaning on the card table and smirking. "Look who I found," he said.

"Wha — " Before I even finished the word, I realized talking to King was a waste of time. "Johnny, are you okay?" I asked.

Johnny threw the airplane and it nosedived to the ground. "Uh-huh."

Uh-huh? I had just been through the worst fifteen minutes of my life, aged about ten years, even began imagining what life in prison would be like — and all he could say was *Uh-huh?*

I felt relieved, but I wanted to kill him.

"Johnny, what happened?" I cried. "Mathew and I couldn't find you in the bathroom! Why didn't you stick with us?"

Johnny shrugged. "Mathew left before me. You left, too."

"I did not!"

King sort of chuckled and shook his head. "Chill out, Logan. He's okay, in case you didn't notice. No thanks to you, though."

I spun around and looked King in the eye. "What do *you* have to do with this? Why don't you mind your own business?"

King backed off, raising his hands defensively. "Hey, if you'd been minding *your* business, I wouldn't have had to bring him back."

"*You* brought him back?" I said.

King nodded nonchalantly. "I saw him coming out the back entrance of the men's room, totally and completely alone. The poor kid looked pretty frightened — "

"*Back* entrance?" I said. "Johnny, when you finished, where did you go?"

"Um, I left the bathroom and went into the hall."

"The hall with the candy machines?" I asked.

"Yeah. And nobody was there . . ."

"I was, too!" Mathew protested.

"Well, *I* didn't see you," Johnny said. "So I went outside."

"When you went outside, did you pass by the machines?" I asked.

Johnny thought a minute. "Uh-uh. I went the other way."

King gave a cocky, I-told-you-so smile. "The back entrance, like I said. So there I was, ready to go home, and this poor kid was just standing there, helpless and lost — "

"Get to the point, King," Kristy said, letting out an exasperated sigh.

"So I brought him here," King said. "It's a good thing I'd seen him before and knew who he was."

"Yeah, because he probably didn't want to talk to you," Kristy said.

"I *don't* go potty," Johnny reminded King.

"Okay, you said that a million times," King replied (sensitive soul that he is).

I forced these words out of my mouth: "Thanks, King." It hurt, but I had to say it.

"Hey, my pleasure," King said. "You girls ever need another member, you know who to call."

With every stupid thing King said, I could feel myself shrinking. But Kristy just sneered at him and said, "Don't push your luck. We have a minimum IQ requirement."

I wished I had thought of that.

"Hmmmph. Some gratitude," King mumbled.

Kristy was only warming up. "Hey, King,"

she said. "I think I hear your mommy calling. Don't you have to go potty?"

Johnny's eyes popped wide open. "*He* goes potty?"

"Only after Lois gets off it," King said. But before Kristy could say another thing, he turned and left, calling, "Ta-ta, girls!" over his shoulder.

As he lumbered away, Mary Anne said, "What a creep."

I stood there, speechless. Johnny and Mathew were playing with paper airplanes as if nothing had happened. A small crowd of people was shuffling away, muttering among themselves. Kristy was staring at me with her arms folded.

I had an urge to run after King and tell him not to mention the incident to anyone. I would *bribe* him if I had to. How could I possibly show up at practice after this? The guys were going to take me to the cleaners. I was going to become the laughingstock of every SMS team. An outcast.

I'd spent my life playing sports, making friends with my teammates — and now it was all going down the tubes.

And all because of the Baby-sitters Club.

I felt Mary Anne's arm around my shoulder. "Don't worry about it," she said. "Everything worked out fine."

For now, I wanted to say. I took a deep breath, looking from Mary Anne to Kristy. I wanted to tell them how I felt, but I couldn't. They had just heard King try to make himself into a hero. I had to tell my side of the story. "I guess I owe you both an explanation."

I told them the entire story — the earlier episode with King and his buddies, Johnny's hurt feelings, the incident at the candy machine. The more I talked, the more I realized how stupid I had been.

"I feel terrible," I said. "This was all my fault. I never should have listened to Johnny. I should have insisted on going inside. And when I *did* finally go inside, I shouldn't have panicked. I should have checked out the building and found the other exit."

"Logan, you're being too hard on yourself," Mary Anne said. "It could have happened to anyone. You meant well. You were just being sensitive to Johnny's feelings."

"I was also being incredibly irresponsible and hysterical," I replied. "I mean, talk about safe sitting! I broke just about every rule."

"You did not, Logan," Kristy said. "Part of good sitting is recognizing what a kid *needs*, right? That's what you were trying to do. We all make mistakes."

"I don't know . . ." So many thoughts were tumbling around in my head. Thoughts of my

114

former friends laughing at me, the panic on Mathew's face as I dragged him around the shopping center, the accusing looks from strangers.

Suddenly the solution to my problem became clear, "Guys, this is ridiculous," I said. "I can't take Dawn's place."

"What?" Kristy said.

"Logan, don't say that," added Mary Anne gently.

But I'd made up my mind. "It just isn't working. I have to resign."

"Look, we can talk it out at Monday's meeting," Kristy said. "Maybe we can find a better way to work around your schedule."

"Kristy, *you* said the club is going to get busier and busier," I said. "It's already out of control. I — I don't even know if I can be an associate member."

Mary Anne was looking at me with those deep, searching eyes. "You really mean it, don't you?"

For a moment I wanted to laugh and say I was joking. I hated to disappoint Mary Anne.

"Can you at least give us another week?" Kristy said. "We're really busy."

I took a deep breath. "No, Kristy," I said. "I can't. You'll have to do without me, starting Monday."

115

CHAPTER 14

"No *girls* at this table!"

King bellowed at his own joke. I calmly put my lunch tray down across from him. "But gorillas are okay?" I asked, handing him a banana from my tray.

Around us, the football team laughed. King scowled. "Get out of here . . . Lois."

I pretended to yawn. "Real clever. How long did it take you to think of that one?"

There was another burst of laughter. I felt pretty good. Insulting people is not my strong point, but I was getting better out of necessity. It was the only way to deal with King.

A week and a half had gone by since the health fair. A week and a half since I'd done any baby-sitting.

I had quit, cold turkey.

The first practice after the fair had been brutal. Insults flew from all over. "Potty animal" was one of the nicer ones. I finally lost it when Irv Hirsch said, "Leave Lois alone! She *couldn't* go into the boys' room at the fair. Girls aren't allowed!"

Instantly a shoving match started, and four other guys jumped in. Coach Mills broke us up and angrily sent the whole team to the showers early.

After that, things became better, little by little. I went to all the practices and worked out just about every day for track tryouts. Most of the guys started laying off me — except for Irv and, of course, King.

As I sat down to eat, I felt a little nervous. The guys were talking about the tryouts, which were scheduled for after school that day.

"What are you guys going out for?" Trevor casually asked the table.

"Pole vault," Harry replied with a mouthful of chicken.

"Low hurdles," Jim Poirier said.

"The hundred-yard dash," King said. "Same as Lois."

As you can see, practically the whole football team had decided to go out for track. Some of those guys were really fast and agile, which made me a little nervous.

I picked at my salad, spearing a plum tomato from the bottom.

"Is that all you're going to eat?" Austin asked.

"Yeah," I said. My tray held only fruit, salad, and soup, as opposed to my usual huge meal. "I don't want to fill up before tryouts."

King nearly choked on his milkshake. "What is this, the new Baby-sitters Club diet?"

"Cram it, King," Austin, Trevor, and I said in perfect unison. That had become sort of a battle chant of ours over the past week or so.

I heard sudden laughter from the Baby-sitters Club table and glanced over. Apparently, Claudia had told a hilarious joke. She was shrugging, a half-wrapped Yankee Doodle in her hand. Mary Anne was leaning back in her chair, looking happy as could be. And Dawn had the darkest tan I'd seen in months.

Yes, Dawn was back. Jeff's recovery had gone well, and she came home after helping throw a party for him.

The truth? I wished I were sitting with them. Quitting the BSC so suddenly had felt a little weird. I actually missed sitting for the Hobart boys. I even missed the meetings, believe it or not.

Since I had quit, most of the BSC members were acting differently toward me. Not exactly *unfriendly*, but just . . . not the same. A little colder, not as open. I had the feeling that if I weren't going out with Mary Anne, they wouldn't talk to me at all.

Still, I knew I'd made the right decision. You know those old-fashioned scales, the ones with two hanging baskets, balanced in the middle like a seesaw? If you put equal weight in both baskets, the scale is balanced. But if you load up too much on one side, you have to load the other to make up for it.

That was how I felt. I had overloaded the baby-sitting side of my life, and now I was loading up on the athletic side. Actually, Mary Anne was the one who thought of describing my life that way. We had had a few long talks about it. She listened patiently and was very supportive. One time, when I started doubting my decision, she said, "Stick to your plan, Logan. It doesn't do anyone much good if you're miserable." If you ask me, that's about as understanding as a person can get.

But you know what? Underneath it all, I could tell she felt hurt by my quitting the BSC.

Oh, well, I guess you can't have a perfect balance all the time, huh?

I was a basket case by the end of that day. All I could think about were the tryouts. I don't remember a thing about my classes, except for the time my stomach let out this humongous growl while we were discussing *The Call of the Wild* in English.

After school ended, I was the first one to reach the locker room. I got dressed, then ran outside and warmed up with a few push-ups and jumping jacks.

Before long, out came the one-man comedy channel. "Hey, I didn't know the girls' team tryouts were today!" was King's cheerful greeting to me.

"Then why did you get dressed up?" I retorted.

Boy, this was getting boring. I suddenly envisioned King tottering up to me at our fiftieth high school reunion and saying, "Who's this girl, eh?"

I decided to take a slow jog around the track, then do a set of stretches. I could see the other guys filing onto the field, the ones who had made my life so awful — Harry, Irv, Jim, Steve, Alex, Bob, and Peter H.

As I said, by then only King and Irv were still razzing me, but here's the weird thing. The minute I saw the others, I felt a shudder. I used to be totally comfortable and secure around these guys, and now I was actually a little *afraid* of them. I still wasn't positive they'd transformed into nice guys again.

In team sports, you always try to attack first and put your opponents on the defensive.

After awhile the losing team's morale breaks down, and they begin defeating themselves.

Well, that's what had been happening to me. The past few weeks had been like a long game, and those guys had figured out how to put me on the defensive.

But guess what. I was not going to defeat myself. Not if I could help it.

"Hey, Lois," Irv said.

"Hi, Irv," I replied cheerfully.

He wasn't expecting that. His face kind of fell, as if *I'd* insulted *him*. I almost laughed.

A few minutes later, the track coach, Mr. Leavitt, blew his whistle and signaled for us to gather around him. "Okay, you've all signed up for your main event," he announced, "but remember, you're going to show me three other events of your choice. I'm interested in well-rounded athletes. You can specialize when you get to high school."

We knew the rules already. In addition to the hundred-yard dash, I had planned on trying the high jump, the low hurdles, and the four-forty.

"Boys," Coach Leavitt said in a fatherly voice, "this is a pretty darn big turnout, and only a few spots are open on the team. I've been watching you work out this week, and I can tell there's a lot of talent here. Which means that some terrific athletes aren't going to make it. Now, I wish I could take you all, but I can't. So instead, I'll wish you all good luck!"

We clapped our thanks. (Secretly I wondered how many times in his career he'd given that speech.)

The pole vault was first. I watched tensely as Harry jumped higher than anyone else. Next was the long jump, and I was so jittery I couldn't even pay attention.

Why? Because the hundred-yard dash was third.

Before I knew it, I was lining up on the track markers with four other guys, including King.

"Your bra strap's showing," King whispered to me.

"Your shoelace is untied," I replied.

It was, too. King knelt down glumly and tied it.

I began psyching myself up. The hundred-yard dash is over before you know it, so everyone runs it flat-out. There's no holding back. If I didn't get a good jump, I'd spend the whole time desperately trying to catch up.

"On your marks!" Coach Leavitt called out.

King sprang to his feet and took his mark.

"Yea, Logan!"

"Go get 'em, mate!"

There was no mistaking those Australian accents. The Hobart boys were in the stands.

"Get set!" the coach yelled out.

"Your cheering section is here, Lois!" King said as he went into his crouch.

Yeah, they were. And it would have bugged the heck out of me a couple of weeks before. But just then, it made me feel *great*.

"Go!"

We shot forward.

I got a decent jump. Instantly, I could feel myself pulling ahead of everyone else.

Except King. For a big guy, he was quick. His legs had tight, powerful muscles — perfect sprinter's legs. He matched me step for step.

The finish line loomed closer. King was pulling ahead.

I tried for a last-minute "kick." I could feel my hamstrings screaming back at me.

"Come on! You can do it!"

"Ya-hoo!"

"Go, Logan!"

That was Mary Anne. And Claudia. And Kristy. And some other voices. It *was* a cheering section!

I could barely feel my legs touch the ground. I flew ahead, seeing only one thing — the red tape across the track, just a few yards ahead.

Thwipppp! It snapped as I passed through.

I felt everything go slack. My legs seemed to take on a life of their own, carrying me another twenty yards or so.

It was over. I had won. And I had beaten King.

Those were the only thoughts in my head.

"He won! He won!"

"Yea!"

Obviously the same went for my "fans."

I looked at the stands for the first time. Sure enough, the entire Baby-sitters Club was there, cheering at the tops of their lungs. The four Hobart boys were with them, as well as Jenny Prezzioso, Charlotte Johanssen, a few of the Pike clan — and Hunter and Kerry.

I thought my cheeks would crack from smiling so much. I waved back.

"Nice job," one of the other runners said to me.

"Thanks," I replied.

King, however, was at a loss for words. He limped to the sidelines, holding his thigh as if he'd pulled it.

I knew beyond a doubt that his thigh was perfectly normal.

I finished third in the high jump and second in the low hurdles, which was better than I had expected. As the last event ended, the sun was starting to set. Coach Leavitt took a few notes, stroked his chin a little, then gestured for us to gather around.

He exhaled, still tugging on his chin. "You're good, all of you," he said. "You make my job tough."

No one said a word. I could feel my heart pounding.

"Okay, here are the fellows I want to see at our first practice." He began reading from his clipboard: "Nolan . . . Stillman . . . Greenberg . . . Saunders . . . Hayes . . . and Bruno. The rest of you, thanks. I encourage you to try again in the spring."

"Yippee!"

"He did it!"

My "cheering section" had heard every word. They jumped up and down, hugging each other and waving at me.

I felt like I was floating ten feet in the air.

A couple of my new teammates, plus some of the other guys, were watching the cheering. With a big smile, Peter Hayes turned to me and said, "Hey, Logan, who's the cute girl?"

"Yeah," Lew Greenberg said, his eyes glued to somebody.

I followed his glance to the stands. Claudia was throwing her head back in a loud victory howl, Kristy was trying to do a "wave" with Mary Anne and Stacey, Dawn was doing a kind of impromptu dance, and Mal and Jessi were jumping around excitedly with a bunch of kids.

I laughed. "Which one?"

Oh well, I guess *some* people found it kind of cool to be cheered on by pretty girls and little kids.

Out of the corner of my eye, I could see Clarence King walking off. He didn't have the slightest trace of a limp, and he kept his head down all the way to the lockers.

After I identified just about every BSC member to my new friends, I ran to the stands. As I approached Mary Anne, the others chattered away and clapped me on the back.

"This was your idea, wasn't it?" I whispered, wrapping Mary Anne in a big bear hug.

"Ooh, not so hard, Logan," she said with a laugh. "I . . . uh, have to go potty."

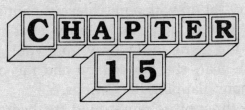

CHAPTER 15

"I don't want to play dinosaurs!" Kerry said. She was bent over some homework on her bedroom desk.

Hunter and I paused at her door, our knees bent, our fingers curved like claws. "You . . . have . . . no . . . choice!" I croaked in a deep voice.

"Be one of us or be eaten!" Hunter said in a high-pitched, stuffed-up version of the same voice.

"Go away!" Kerry protested, although I could see her lips starting to curl into a tiny smile.

"What do you think, Allo?" I said to Hunter.

"Let's get her, Tyranno!" Hunter replied.

"*Rrrowwrgh!*" we yelled, pouncing into her room.

"Aaah! Stop! *Stop!*" Kerry screamed.

She giggled as I lifted her out of her seat

and dumped her onto her bed. "Human meat! Yummy!" Hunter said.

"Okay! I'm a dinosaur! *I'm a dinosaur!*" Kerry squealed.

"What kind?" Hunter demanded.

Kerry sat up with a mischievous glint in her eye. "A pterodactyl, and you can't get me because I'm going to fly away from you!"

With that, she hopped up and ran out of her room, flapping her "wings."

The three of us ran around the bedrooms, laughing and roaring and squawking. From downstairs, my mom called, "What on earth are you all doing?"

"Let's get *her*!" Hunter cried.

We stomped downstairs, claws at the ready. "Be one of us or be eaten!" Hunter demanded.

Mom laughed and shook her head. "If I become one of you, you won't be eating *anything* tonight. Your father and I have work to do, and you dinosaurs are welcome to help."

Freshly thawed chicken breasts and spare ribs were gleaming on the kitchen counter. Next to them stood containers of molasses, vinegar, hot peppers, honey, tomatoes, and all the other ingredients for the world-famous Bruno barbecue sauce. My mouth started to water.

"I'll help!" Kerry said.

"Me too!" Hunter said.

Suddenly a strong memory rushed into my brain. A memory of a recent family barbecue that I had almost missed.

I looked at the kitchen clock. It was 5:26. In precisely four minutes, Kristy would be announcing "Order!" and a Friday Baby-sitters Club meeting would begin.

"Hey, Mom?" I said. "Would it be all right if I disappeared for a half hour before dinner?"

"Where are you going?" she asked.

"To a BSC meeting."

"I thought you quit, Logan."

"I did. But . . . I don't know. I just feel like surprising them."

My mom turned to see Kerry carefully measuring molasses into a bowl and Hunter watching intently. "Well, I guess I'm not short on helpers. Just be back as soon as you can."

"Thanks!" I said.

I called Claudia's house. "Baby-sitters Club," said Kristy's voice.

"Hi, it's Logan," I said. "Mind if I come to the meeting? You know, for old time's sake?"

"Well, you better hurry," Kristy said. "It's 5:27."

Typical.

"Great! See you!"

I rushed out of the house, hopped onto my bike, and pedaled to headquarters. I walked into Claudia's room at 5:32.

"You're late!" Kristy snapped.

I stood there in silence for a moment, and then everybody broke into giggles. "What are you doing here, Logan?" Stacey asked.

"I wanted to hang out with the *girls*," I said, in my best football-jock voice.

"Great!" Dawn said.

"Have a seat," Kristy ordered. She gave Dawn a sharp look. "Dawwnnn . . ."

"Oops." Dawn hopped off the bed and sat on the floor, leaving a spot beside Mary Anne.

"You didn't have to do that," I said.

"Oh, yes she did," Mary Anne snapped.

Everyone cracked up again. As I sat down next to Mary Anne, Kristy said, "Any new business?"

"I talked to Jeff today," Dawn replied.

"Yeah? How is he?"

"He said — and I'm serious — 'It only hurts when I laugh.' "

"How many jokes did you tell him?" Claudia asked.

"I tried not to tell any, but we ended up laughing anyway," Dawn said. "Every once in a while he would say, 'Owww!' I felt like such a rotten sister."

"But he's going to be okay?" Stacey said.

"The doctor told him he'll be playing tennis again in two weeks," Dawn replied. "And you know what Jeff said? 'Fantastic! Who's going to teach me?' "

We groaned.

"That's Jeff," Mallory said.

Rrrring!

Claudia picked up the receiver. "Baby-sitters Club! Oh, hi!" She gave me a quick glance. "Uh, no . . . Yes, I know. It is too bad, but I'm sure one of us is available. I'll call you right back . . . Okay, 'bye."

She hung up.

"Who was that?" Jessi asked.

"Just Mrs. Hobart," Claudia said. "Who's free Wednesday at four o'clock?"

Mary Anne looked in the record book. "Let's see . . ."

It is too bad, but I'm sure one of us is available was what Claudia had said to Mrs. Hobart. I knew she must have been talking about me. Boy, did I feel a pang of guilt. I was letting the Hobart boys down.

Part of me wanted to say, "I'll do it," but I stopped myself. On Wednesday at four, I was going to be at track practice.

I wasn't going to miss it, and not because I was afraid of teasing. Track was just more important to me than sitting, that's all. The scales were starting to balance, and I didn't want to tip them the other way.

Scales.

Suddenly those dumb scales were making me think about sports, about the BSC, about me . . .

"Dawn, you're free," Mary Anne said. "And you, too, Jessi."

"It's okay with me if Dawn takes it," Jessi said. "She has some catching up to do."

"Thanks," Dawn said, smiling.

Claudia called Mrs. Hobart back, and the date was set.

"I heard the Hobart boys really liked you," Dawn said to me as Claudia hung up.

"I liked them, too," I answered.

"Ben says his brothers are really upset they'll never see you again," Mal said.

"Who says I won't?"

"Well, I mean, if you're not sitting, it'll be hard," Mal replied. "As it is, with your sports and, you know, dating Mary Anne sometimes . . ."

Mary Anne laughed. "Sometimes!"

"Who says I won't be sitting?" I repeated.

That stopped the conversation cold.

Finally Kristy said, "Earth to Logan! You quit the BSC, remember?"

I nodded. "I know. Does that have to stick for life?"

Mary Anne sat forward. Kristy scratched her head. Mal and Jessi exchanged a glance.

"Logan, what are you saying?" Mary Anne asked.

"Well," I said, "I guess what I'm saying is, will you guys let me be an associate member again?"

Kristy grinned. "You mean it?"

"I *knew* it!" Mary Anne cried.

"Wait a minute," Stacey said. "Why did you change your mind?"

I thought for a moment. "Well, first of all, I miss sitting," I said. "Being a *regular* member was messing me up, not being an associate. Besides, the scales are balancing, but I don't want them to tip the *other* way . . ."

"Huh?" Claudia said.

I gave Mary Anne a Look. She knew what I was talking about.

"Here's another reason," I went on. "I've finally figured out how to deal with King and his gang. They don't bother me at all anymore." I smiled. "In fact, some of you guys may be getting phone calls from them."

Claudia's eyes popped open and she gasped. "Lew Greenberg!" she exclaimed. "Which one is he?"

"Taller than me, thin, dark hair, friendly smile," I said.

"Like, really handsome, with dimples?" Claudia asked.

I shrugged. That wasn't the way I saw him, but . . . "Yeah, I guess so."

"Aaaagh!" she cried. "*That's* who that was! The cute guy who was pointing to me after your tryouts! He called me and asked me out, but I hung up on him because I thought he was playing a joke!"

"Uh-oh," Stacey said. "Scratch that one."

"No wonder he looked so depressed at the last practice," I commented.

"Really?" Claudia said, wide-eyed.

"He told me those tears were because of contact lenses," I added.

"Really?"

I couldn't help it. I started to laugh.

Claudia narrowed her eyes and started hitting me with a Fritos bag. "Oh, you liar!"

"Stop! Stop!" I shouted. "Seriously, Claudia, don't worry! I'll talk to him. I promise!"

Claudia and I declared a truce, and the rest of the meeting passed quietly — a few phone calls, a little gossip, then six o'clock.

Mary Anne and I left together. "I'm glad you came to the meeting," she said.

"I am, too. And I'm glad you all want me back."

It was true. I felt as if a huge load had been lifted from my back. And I was confident things would work out.

"Hi, Logan!" a voice shouted from across the street.

Hoi, Low-gin! Only one family I knew talked like that — the Hobarts.

I turned to see Johnny and Mathew running across their lawn toward the street.

My baby-sitting instincts took over. "Stay there!" I called out.

I began to cross the street, but Mary Anne grabbed my hand. "Don't go!" she said. "Look who's coming."

I could see King, Pete Black, Harry Nolan, and Steve Randazzo in the distance on their bikes. "Don't worry," I told her.

Then I ran toward the Hobart house, shouting, "Tickle monster!"

Immediately, Johnny and Mathew ran away, giggling like crazy. I scooped them up, and then tumbled to the ground with them. They squirmed and squirmed, trying to tickle me before I could tickle them. (I let them, of course.)

I could hear the metallic buzzing of the four ten-speed bikes as my teammates approached. I could also see Mary Anne cringing, expecting some typical insult.

"Hi, Logan!" Harry called out.

"Hey, Mathew . . . Johnny-boy," King said.

A moment later they had rounded the corner and were out of sight. Mary Anne turned toward me, a grin on her face.

I smiled back. Everything was going to work out.

Johnny was standing at the edge of the lawn, looking up the street with his hands on his hips. "I *hate* that name!" he said, his chin in the air. "It's *Johnny*, not Johnny-boy."

I couldn't hold back a laugh. Well, *almost* everything was going to work out, anyway.

About the Author

ANN M. MARTIN did *a lot* of baby-sitting when she was growing up in Princeton, New Jersey. She is a former editor of books for children, and was graduated from Smith College.

Ms. Martin lives in New York City with her cats, Mouse and Rosie. She likes ice cream and *I Love Lucy*; and she hates to cook.

Ann Martin's Apple Paperbacks include *Yours Turly, Shirley; Ten Kids, No Pets; With You and Without You; Bummer Summer;* and all the other books in the Baby-sitters Club series.

THE BABY-SITTERS CLUB®

by Ann M. Martin

More titles... ▶

The Baby-sitters Club titles continued...

❏ MG42508-0	#35 **Stacey and the Mystery of Stoneybrook**	$2.95
❏ MG43565-5	#36 **Jessi's Baby-sitter**	$2.95
❏ MG43566-3	#37 **Dawn and the Older Boy**	$3.25
❏ MG43567-1	#38 **Kristy's Mystery Admirer**	$3.25
❏ MG43568-X	#39 **Poor Mallory!**	$3.25
❏ MG44082-9	#40 **Claudia and the Middle School Mystery**	$3.25
❏ MG43570-1	#41 **Mary Anne Versus Logan**	$2.95
❏ MG44083-7	#42 **Jessi and the Dance School Phantom**	$3.25
❏ MG43572-8	#43 **Stacey's Emergency**	$3.25
❏ MG43573-6	#44 **Dawn and the Big Sleepover**	$2.95
❏ MG43574-4	#45 **Kristy and the Baby Parade**	$3.25
❏ MG43569-8	#46 **Mary Anne Misses Logan**	$3.25
❏ MG44971-0	#47 **Mallory on Strike**	$3.25
❏ MG43571-X	#48 **Jessi's Wish**	$3.25
❏ MG44970-2	#49 **Claudia and the Genius of Elm Street**	$3.25
❏ MG44969-9	#50 **Dawn's Big Date**	$3.25
❏ MG44968-0	#51 **Stacey's Ex-Best Friend**	$3.25
❏ MG44966-4	#52 **Mary Anne + 2 Many Babies**	$3.25
❏ MG44967-2	#53 **Kristy for President**	$3.25
❏ MG44965-6	#54 **Mallory and the Dream Horse**	$3.25
❏ MG44964-8	#55 **Jessi's Gold Medal**	$3.25
❏ MG45575-3	**Logan's Story Special Edition Readers' Request**	$3.25
❏ MG44240-6	**Baby-sitters on Board! Super Special #1**	$3.50
❏ MG44239-2	**Baby-sitters' Summer Vacation Super Special #2**	$3.50
❏ MG43973-1	**Baby-sitters' Winter Vacation Super Special #3**	$3.50
❏ MG42493-9	**Baby-sitters' Island Adventure Super Special #4**	$3.50
❏ MG43575-2	**California Girls! Super Special #5**	$3.50
❏ MG43576-0	**New York, New York! Super Special #6**	$3.50
❏ MG44963-X	**Snowbound Super Special #7**	$3.50

Available wherever you buy books...or use this order form.

Scholastic Inc., P.O. Box 7502, 2931 E. McCarty Street, Jefferson City, MO 65102

Please send me the books I have checked above. I am enclosing $_____
(please add $2.00 to cover shipping and handling). Send check or money order - no
cash or C.O.D.s please.

Name _____

Address _____

City_____ State/Zip _____

Please allow four to six weeks for delivery. Offer good in the U.S. only. Sorry, mail orders are not
available to residents of Canada. Prices subject to change.

BSC991